"Marriage."

She stared up at him, into those unreadable eyes. "What?"

"We're going to be married. Tomorrow." His words were clipped. She thought, crazily, that they might have been arranging a dental appointment. "At noon."

She waited for him to laugh. When he didn't, she gave one bark of hysterical laughter for the both of them.

"You're crazy."

He grabbed her arm as she turned away and spun her toward him. "It's the only solution," he said coldly. "My son is going to have two parents. A father, and a mother."

THE BARONS

**Four brothers:
bonded by inheritance, battling for love!**

Jonas Baron is approaching his eighty-fifth
birthday. He has ruled Espada, his sprawling
estate in Texas hill country, for more than
forty years, but now he admits it's time he
chose an heir.

Jonas has three sons—Gage, Travis and Slade,
all ruggedly handsome and each with a successful
business empire of his own; none wishes to give
up the life he's fought for to take over Espada.
Jonas also has a stepdaughter; beautiful and
spirited, Caitlin loves the land as much as he
does, but she's not of the Baron blood.

So who will receive Baron's bequest? As Gage,
Travis, Slade and Caitlin discover, there's more at
stake than just Espada. For love also has its part
to play in deciding their futures....

Sit back now and enjoy Slade's story,
and be sure to look out next for
The Taming of Tyler Kincaid.
In this sensational, longer, value-read, Caitlin
finally meets her match in the mysterious Tyler.
But is he Jonas's long-lost son, the fourth Baron
brother? Available February (#2081),
in Harlequin Presents®

SANDRA MARTON

Slade Baron's Bride

THE BARONS

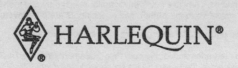

HARLEQUIN®

TORONTO • NEW YORK • LONDON
AMSTERDAM • PARIS • SYDNEY • HAMBURG
STOCKHOLM • ATHENS • TOKYO • MILAN • MADRID
PRAGUE • WARSAW • BUDAPEST • AUCKLAND

ISBN 0-373-12063-X

SLADE BARON'S BRIDE

First North American Publication 1999.

Copyright © 1999 by Sandra Myles.

Visit us at www.romance.net

Printed in U.S.A.

CHAPTER ONE

SLADE BARON figured the blonde in the green suede suit had to know that her skirt fell open each time she crossed her legs.

They were fine-looking legs, too. Long, tanned and trim.

He was waiting out a weather delay in East Coast Air's first-class lounge and he'd noticed her when she'd first entered, about half an hour ago. Every man in the room had noticed her. They'd have to have been neutered, to ignore a woman that desirable, especially when there was nothing else to look at besides the rain, pelting against the window.

As beautiful as she was, she looked completely business-like, carrying a computer case in one hand and a carry-on in the other, the same as almost everyone else who was waiting out the summer storm. But then she sat down, right opposite Slade, took a book from the outside pocket of her carry-on, crossed her legs...and the proper-looking suede skirt revealed a slit that went straight up to her thighs.

She knew it, too. She crossed, and recrossed those long, gorgeous legs damned near every two minutes. And Slade was in just the right place to admire the view.

Every other man in hailing distance was doing the same thing. Why wouldn't they? There was no point in staring out at the rain, or at the bolts of lightning that sizzled across the charcoal sky. Looking at the Departure Board wasn't much better. Delayed, delayed, delayed, was what it said, what it would say until the storm passed over.

Slade had already gone through the notes for his presentation, read the Business section of the *Boston Globe,* phoned Edwin Dobbs at the Beaufort Trust in Baltimore. It was either watch Blondie or go nuts with boredom.

Blondie was the winner, hands down.

She looked up from her book, caught Slade's frankly appraising glance and smiled. He smiled back. She put her head down again, flipped a page, then gently slid one leg against the other. The skirt fell open another couple of inches. Slade folded his arms, narrowed his eyes, settled back and let his imagination take over.

What did the skirt still conceal?

Black lace, probably. He'd known a lot of women in his thirty years, more than his fair share, his brothers said teasingly, and he was sure that Blondie was the black lace type. On the other hand, a delicate pink would look great against that tan.

Those long legs scissored, and there it was. Black lace, just a flash, but enough to make the guy sitting a couple of chairs away groan. The poor sap covered it well, changing the groan to a cough, but Blondie knew.

She lifted her head, looked straight at the guy, then at Slade. She smiled. He smiled. And when she repeated the I'm-wearing-lace-panties routine, Slade picked up his computer case and his carry-on bag, rose from his chair, started toward her...

And stopped. Just stopped, halfway across the floor.

The blonde's brows lifted. She waited. Hell, he could feel everybody waiting, watching, trying to figure out what was going on. A man would have to be comatose not to have understood the invitation, and dead not to accept it.

Slade wasn't comatose or dead, but he was going to pass. He hadn't known it until a second ago but now he did, the same as he knew it was his only choice. Memory had deadened the pleasant sense of anticipation and turned it to anger. Not at the blonde, or the weather.

Slade's anger was at himself.

Frowning, he strode past the blonde, who looked after him with a sigh of disappointment. He went past the reception desk where some bozo with a loud voice and a red face was bitching about missing his flight, out the door and into the general waiting area.

Ahead, through the windows, he could see flight 435 to Baltimore squatting beside its gate like some big, wet gray bird. People milled around. It was noisy, crowded and not even the air conditioning could keep up with the heat and humidity.

Slade kept on walking, straight through the building, until he reached the end of the corridor. He stopped, stared out the window again and told himself to stop being an idiot.

"It was eighteen months ago," he muttered. "A year and a half. And that's as good as forever, in any man's life."

A muscle knotted in his cheek. He put his computer and his carry-on at his feet, pulled his cellular phone from his pocket and called his office.

"It's me," he said when his secretary answered. "Any messages?"

There were none but he hadn't really expected any, considering that he'd phoned only half an hour or so earlier. He disconnected, started to punch in the number for the Beaufort Trust but stopped when he realized he'd just done that only a little while ago, too. He picked up his computer, started to look for a public phone and changed his mind. There were probably no urgent e-mails, either.

He took the nearest chair, sighed and turned on the machine.

Solitaire would eat up some time. It always gave him a laugh, how many well-dressed business types sat hunched over their computers on a long flight, playing endless hands of the game.

He could be industrious, call up his designs for the new world headquarters the Beaufort Conglomerate wanted him to build in Baltimore.

Or he could just stop being an idiot and deal with reality.

Slade frowned, switched off the computer and put it away.

What had happened in Denver was old news. There was

no reason all those memories should have come flooding back. The blonde with the slit skirt was nothing like Lara, nothing at all. And even if the situations were similar—the weather delay, the first-class lounge, a man and a woman just looking to kill some time—even if all that was the same, it wouldn't have ultimately ended the same way.

A year and a half later, he wouldn't be sitting around, remembering what had happened, and wondering why in hell he should still be remembering it at all.

"Dammit, Baron," Slade said, through his teeth.

A man standing nearby shot him a funny look, picked up his suitcase and moved away. Slade couldn't blame him. Guys who sat around airports, looking out at the weather and talking to themselves, were guys sane people avoided.

He wondered what the man with the suitcase would think if he walked over and said, Listen, pal, there's nothing wrong with me. It's just that I picked up this babe a long time back. We had a night of mind-blowing sex, and I still can't get her out of my head.

Which was crazy. One hundred percent, loony-tunes crazy. Because the whole incident had been nothing. A meaningless one-night stand. Meaningless, Slade thought, and stared out at the rain.

But it wasn't rain he saw. What he saw, in his mind, was snow.

Snow, heavy and thick, each flake the size of a five-cent coin. Snow had begun falling from the leaden Colorado sky to blanket the field on that December morning. His plane had made an unscheduled landing because another storm had put a monkey wrench into the schedule of every airline flying east of Denver.

He'd been sitting out the delay in yet another handsome, anonymous, first-class lounge.

An hour delay, the voice over the loudspeaker kept repeating, even after the hour had stretched to two and then three. The storm hadn't been expected but it wasn't anything to worry about. Things would be back on schedule as fast as East Coast Air could manage.

Except the snow kept falling, and the sky got darker and darker. And Slade's impatience grew.

He was heading home to Boston after a long weekend's visit to his brother in California. It had been a great couple of days filled with laughs and volleyball along the beach outside Travis's Malibu house. Trav, dependable, as always had even lined up Saturday night dates that had been world-class.

Now, Slade had thought, sitting in the lounge and stewing, now, he was going to ruin that good time by spending Sunday evening snowbound, trapped at Denver International.

He'd sighed, told himself to stop being a jerk. The freaky storm was nobody's fault. He was a pilot, had been since he was a kid. He, of all people, knew that sometimes there was no arguing with the weather.

The key to getting through this without going nuts was finding something to do. He'd already checked his e-mail. He'd read *Time* from cover to cover. What next? he thought wearily…

And then he saw the woman sitting across from him.

He figured she must have come into the lounge in the last few minutes, while he was reading. Otherwise, he'd have noticed her the same way every man in the room had noticed her. They were all trying to be casual, giving her cautious looks from behind their newspapers, but Slade had never believed in being cautious about anything.

Besides, a woman like this deserved a man's complete attention.

Her hair was somewhere between gold and red. Strawberry blond, probably, but it seemed a tame way to describe a color that reminded him of early autumn mornings. He couldn't see her eyes—she was looking down at the portable computer in her lap—but he had the feeling they'd be a deep blue. She was wearing what he'd heard women refer to as a man-tailored suit, very proper and demure, but it didn't look all that demure on her, not even the skirt, which hung primly to her crossed knees.

He could sense her irritation as she poked at her computer. It was the same brand as his, he noticed. She said something under her breath, looked up—and he saw not just her eyes, as deep a blue as he'd imagined, but a face as spectacular as any that had ever been in his dreams.

Slade didn't hesitate. He picked up his things, walked the few feet to her and grinned.

"Here you go, darlin'," he said.

The look she gave him would have turned the snow outside to ice. "I beg your pardon?"

He smiled, gave the guy sitting in the next chair a pointed look and nodded his thanks when the man fidgeted a couple of seconds, then got up and moved off.

"I," Slade said, settling into the newly vacated seat, "am the answer to your prayers, Sugar."

Her eyes turned even colder. "I am not named 'Sugar.'" She looked him up and down, her pretty mouth curling with disdain. "You're out of your league, cowboy. If those boots of yours are made for walking, you'd better let them walk."

"Ah," he said wisely, "I see. You think this is just an old-fashioned pickup."

"My goodness." The woman batted her lashes. They were dark, thick and impossibly long. "And you're going to try to tell me it isn't, is that right?"

Slade sighed, shook his head, opened his computer case and took out his spare battery.

"It's painful to be misjudged, Sugar." He held out the battery, his expression one of wide-eyed innocence. "You need a battery for your computer and I just happen to have an extra. Now, does that sound like a pickup line to you?"

She looked back at him for what seemed forever. Just when he thought she was going to send him packing, he saw the corner of her mouth twitch.

"Yes," she said.

"Well, you're right," he said. "But you have to admit, it's creative."

She laughed, and he laughed, and that was the way it all began.

"Hi," he said, and held out his hand. "I'm Slade."

She hesitated, then took his hand. "I'm Lara."

Lara. It seemed just right for this woman. Soft, feminine, yet with a certain strength to it. It was a pleasant contradiction in terms, just like her handshake, which was strong, almost masculine. Still, her fingers were long and delicate, and her hand seemed lost in his.

A tiny electric jolt passed between them.

"Static electricity," she said quickly, and pulled back her hand.

"Sure," Slade said, but he didn't think so. And, from the flush that rose in her lovely face, he didn't think she thought so, either.

"I couldn't help but overhear your, uh, your conversation." He smiled. "The one you were having with yourself. I didn't actually hear what you called your dead battery, but I have a pretty good imagination."

She laughed. "I'm afraid I wasn't being very polite."

"I'm serious about giving you that extra battery."

"Thanks, but I can do without it."

"Well, I'll lend it to you, then. So you can finish up whatever you were doing."

"It's the 'whatever' part that I was going for this time." She smiled, and he told himself he'd never known that a woman's smile could light a room until now. "I was going to play a game of solitaire."

Slade grinned. "Computer solitaire. The wonder of the age. One card or three?"

"One, of course," Lara said primly. "Timed, with Vegas rules."

"The deck with the palm trees?"

She laughed. "Uh-huh. I like that little face that appears, the one that grins when you least expect it."

"Try getting a regular deck of cards to grin at you," Slade said, and they both laughed and began to talk, bouncing from topic to topic as strangers usually do, except he wasn't really sure what he said, or what she said.

He was too busy watching the play of emotion on her face when she laughed, the way she had of widening her eyes when he said something amusing. He was too busy listening to her voice, which was husky and soft and sexy as hell, even though he had the feeling she didn't know it was sexy any more than she knew that little way she had of pushing her hair back from her ear was starting to make him have to curl his hand into a fist to keep from reaching out and doing it himself.

Up close, the suit was still demure but now that he could see a hint of the body beneath it, he knew he'd never think of a suit the same way again. And her scent. Lilacs, he thought. Or maybe lilies of the valley.

"...don't you think?" she said, and Slade nodded and said yes, he definitely did, and hoped he was saying yes to the right thing, because he hadn't heard the question. He told himself he was being ridiculous, to get his jaw off the floor and his brain into gear.

"That's why I think of it as The Dead Battery Conspiracy," Lara said. "You know. You do all the right things, keep their batteries charged—"

Oh, yes, Slade thought, while he kept smiling like an idiot, yes, indeed, there was nothing like keeping your batteries charged.

"You turn them on carefully—"

Carefully? Hell, he didn't want to be turned on carefully. He wanted to scoop her up, drag her off into a dark corner and ravish that mouth and that body.

"—but they don't work. They never do, when you want them to."

"No," Slade finally said, and cleared his throat and changed the topic before he made a spectacle of himself in public.

They talked some more. Or, rather, he talked. She just listened. After a while, he noticed a strange look on her face. He wondered if he was boring her but then he realized it wasn't that. She looked...contemplative. Yeah, that was the word. She smiled in all the right places but he had the feeling she was weighing the consequences of something important, and that whatever it was, it was beyond his comprehension.

It gave him a funny feeling, one he didn't like. So he stopped, in the middle of a sentence, and said, "How about some coffee?"

Lara blinked. She looked back at the coffee bar, then at him.

"Yes," she said finally. "Yes, I'd like that."

He rose from his chair. She did, too. They walked to the rear of the lounge, poured some coffee, sat down on a small sofa in a corner and went on with their conversation about inconsequential things. Weather, and flying, and how some airports were better than others, but all the while they were chatting, he knew it was only a cover for what was really happening between them.

They were turning each other on.

That little shot of electricity came again, when he refilled her cup. Their hands brushed, and the resultant spark made them jump.

"Whoops," she said, with a little laugh, "one of us needs to be grounded before we go up in flames."

"Oh, I don't know," Slade said, with a smile. "Going up in flames might be fun."

Their eyes met and held, and then she looked away and they talked about carpets and static electricity, about everything but the tension stretching between them.

He told himself it was nothing unusual. He was a man who enjoyed women. He always had, ever since the divorced wife of a neighboring rancher back home in Texas had decided to give him herself as a gift for his sixteenth birthday. He liked women, liked the way they sounded and looked and moved. And women liked him. So yeah, he'd sat in a bar, or gone to a party, he'd looked at a woman and she at him and bam, the connection had clicked and the both of them had known they were going to end up in bed together.

But, dammit, this was different. Who was he trying to kid? He wanted this woman with a need that was almost painful. He wanted her in his arms, wanted the scent of her arousal on his skin, the taste of her on his tongue, the hot wetness of her closing around him.

And she wanted him. He could read the signs. The glow in her eyes. The rosy color in her cheeks. The way her coffee cup trembled in her hand. He wondered when she'd be ready to admit it to herself and what he could possibly do about it when she did, considering that they were trapped in this damned lounge with the rest of the world.

"...of the world," Lara said.

"What?"

"I said, it seems as if we're trapped in here, and the world has come to a stop."

"Yes." Slade nodded. "Yes, it does."

They both fell silent. He saw the way she looked at him, from under her lashes, and how she looked away, and he knew it was time.

"You're beautiful," he said softly.

Color flooded her face but she smiled. "Thank you."

"What does your hair look like, when it's loose?"

He saw a pulse flutter in the hollow of her throat. "What?"

"Your hair. Is it long? Does it fall over your shoulders, and your breasts?" He took the cup from her and put it on the table beside him. "This isn't just another pickup line," he said. "You know it's not."

He looked into her eyes and what he saw made his body harden. She knew what he was thinking, that he was imagining what it would be like to strip her of that oh-so-proper suit, take down that carefully tied-back hair, touch her and kiss her until she cried out with need for him.

And in the middle of all those crazy thoughts, another announcement blared from the public-address system.

All flights were grounded, for at least the next few hours. Passengers who wished to secure overnight arrangements were to come up to the desk.

Lara cleared her throat. "Well," she said, and gave a forced laugh, "well, that's that."

She was right. It was over, and he was glad. Whatever insanity had been going on between them was finished.

"Yes." He smiled politely. "Are you going to wait it out here or try for a hotel?"

"Here, I think. How about you?"

"I'll hang in here," he started to say, but he never finished the sentence. "The hell with this," he growled. "Come with me."

Something flashed in her eyes and he thought, for a heartbeat, she was going to say yes.

"No," she whispered. "I can't."

He looked at her left hand, saw no ring. "Are you married?" She shook her head. "Engaged?" She shook her head again. Slade moved closer, until they were a breath apart. "Neither am I. We won't be hurting anyone." He reached out and took her hand. She let him do it, though he felt the tremor in her fingers. "Come to bed with me, Lara."

The color rose in her face. "I can't."

"We'll be incredible together," he said, his hand tightening on hers.

She shook her head. "I—I don't even know you."

"Yes, you do. You've known me forever, the same as I've known you." His voice was rough and low. "As for the details...I'm an architect. I live in Boston. I'm straight, I'm not married, not committed to anyone. I'm twenty-eight years old, I just had my annual physical and my doctor says I'm healthy enough to outlive Methuselah. What more do you need to know, except that I've never wanted a woman as much as I want you?''

And then—he'd never forgotten this—and then she'd looked at him, and something in that blue gaze changed. He'd felt as if he were being evaluated, not only as a man coming on to a woman but in some way he couldn't figure out. She looked at him with that strange expression on her face, the way she had an hour or so before.

It made him uneasy, but the uneasiness was swept aside by a hot rush of longing when she touched the tip of her tongue to her lips.

"It's—it's crazy. Even talking like this—"

He lay a finger lightly against her mouth. He wanted to kiss her instead but touching her was all he dared to do in this public place without losing what little remained of his control.

"I'll get a taxi. There's a hotel not far from here where I've stayed before. They know me. They'll find us a room."

"A taxi. And a hotel, in weather like this?" She made a little sound that might have been a laugh. "You're very sure of yourself, Slade."

"If I were sure of myself," he said softly, "I wouldn't be holding my breath while I wait for your answer."

He could still remember the moment. The noise, all around them. The shuffle of feet and the press of bodies, as weary travelers headed for the desk, or laid claim to chairs and couches. And, in the middle of the confusion, her silence. The tilt of her head, as she looked up at him. That unreadable something, back in her eyes.

"Yes," she said. Just that one word, but it was enough.

He had no memory of leaving the lounge, or of flagging down a taxi. He could hardly recall the ride to the hotel, he only remembered stepping through the doors, his arm hard around her waist, and telling her that he had to leave her for a moment while he made a quick stop at the drugstore in the lobby.

"No," she said, looking up at him. "It's not necessary."

He remembered, too, the first shot of pleasure he'd felt at those words, knowing there'd be no barrier of latex between them…and then the surprisingly harsh jolt of anger when he realized that she took care of her own birth control needs because she had sexual relationships apart from the one she was about to have with him.

It was more than anger he felt. It was the sharp bite of primitive male possessiveness. But by then they were in the room with the door closed on the rest of the world, and he stopped thinking and reached for her.

She panicked. "No!" Her voice quavered. "I'm sorry, Slade. I can't do this."

He framed her face in his hands. "Just kiss me," he whispered. "Kiss me once, and I swear, if you want to leave, I won't try to stop you."

She didn't move, she just looked up at him through wide, fear-filled eyes. He thought of something he'd stumbled upon years ago, back home at Espada. A stallion had broken loose from his stall and trapped a mare. He remembered the arch of the stallion's neck, the wild, rolling eyes. And he remembered the mare's terror, and how that terror had suddenly become something else, once the stallion came over her.

"Lara," he whispered. Slowly, carefully, watching the wary apprehension in her eyes, he lowered his mouth to hers and kissed her. It was difficult, holding himself in check, but he did it, brushing his lips over hers until her mouth warmed and opened beneath his.

"Slade," she sighed, and the sound of his name on her lips made him groan.

His arms swept around her and he gathered her close. She rose toward him, looped her arms around his neck, buried her hands in his hair.

"Please," she said, "oh please, please, please…"

And then he was carrying her to the bed, undressing her, letting down that glorious hair and doing everything he'd wanted, everything she'd wanted, and more.

The storm became a blizzard. It raged across the mountains all that day and night. And they spent all those minutes and hours in bed.

It was like a dream. Lara, in his arms. Her scent, on his skin. The warmth of her, curled against him whenever they dropped into exhausted sleep. He told himself how lucky he was, that making love with this beautiful stranger while a winter storm raged outside would be an incredible memory in years to come.

Toward dawn, something—the moan of the wind, perhaps—awakened him. Lara was asleep in the curve of his arm. He watched her and thought about how, when the storm ended, they'd go their separate ways. She lived in Atlanta, and she was an auditor. That was all she'd told him about herself. He thought, too, of the way she'd made it clear he didn't have to worry about condoms and the angry feeling because she had a life he knew nothing about ripped through him again.

He tried to imagine her leading that life, living in a house he'd never seen, laughing with friends he didn't know. Dating men he didn't want to think about. Lying in arms that weren't his.

Something tightened around his heart. He woke her with kisses, and with the touch of his hand on her breast.

"Lara," he whispered.

Her eyes opened and she smiled sleepily. "Slade? What is it?"

What, indeed? She lived in the South, he in the Northeast. What was he going to say? That he'd fly down to see her every weekend? He didn't see *any* woman every weekend. Well, yeah, he'd been known to establish relationships that lasted a couple of months, but getting involved with a woman who lived in the same city wasn't like getting involved with one who lived hundreds of miles away.

"Leave a toothbrush here," she'd say, "and some clothes." And then she'd expect him to show up on Fridays instead of Saturdays, and leave on Monday instead of

Sunday, and who knew? Sooner or later, maybe she'd say, "You know, I've been thinking that I could move up to Boston..."

"Slade?" Lara curved her hand around his stubbled jaw. "What's the matter?" She smiled. "You look like a little boy who just found out there really isn't a Santa Claus."

He forced a smile to his lips and said he'd been hearing snowplows for a while now, that the roads were probably clear. And that he'd been thinking how terrific this had been and how he hoped that someday, if they could work out the details, they might find the time to get together again.

"Ah," she said, after the barest hesitation, "yes, that sounds good."

He wondered if he'd hurt her feelings but she lifted her mouth to his and kissed him. She touched him. She made him wild for her and he rolled her beneath him and took her again. When it was over, he lay holding her close. He thought of how much he wanted more of this, more of her. It didn't have to be *every* weekend.

He smiled, brought her face to his, and gave her a slow, tender kiss.

"I don't know your address," he said softly, "or your phone number."

And she smiled and stroked a lock of hair back from his eyes.

"I'll write it all down," she whispered, "in the morning."

But when he awoke, in the morning, it was to sunshine, the sound of snowplows and cars and jet engines screaming overhead—and to an empty place in the bed.

Lara was gone. No note. No message. He didn't even know her last name.

She'd run out on him while he slept, and he'd been furious. He'd tried telling himself she had no way of knowing he'd wanted more than the one night, but it didn't take away the feeling that he'd been—well, that somehow, he'd been used.

What he *did* know was that what he'd felt making love to her, the sense that something special was happening, had been his imagination. Sex with a beautiful stranger, every man's fantasy, was all it had been. And, as he'd flown home, he'd thought about how this wasn't just going to be a great memory, it would be one hell of a story. I got snowed in in Denver, he'd say, and I ended up in bed with this incredibly hot babe for almost two days.

Except, he never told that story, not to his partners or even to his brothers. And now, all these months later, he was standing at the window in an airport terminal and wondering why he should still dream about the weekend and the woman because he did, dammit, he dreamed about her, about how it had been to make love to her, the stranger with the soft, sweet mouth and the deep blue eyes. He remembered how she'd felt, in his arms. The little sounds she'd made when he moved inside her, when she arched toward him, wrapped her legs around him...

"Ladies and gentlemen, we're pleased to announce that we are now boarding all flights."

Slade dropped back into reality, realized he was a long way from his gate and ran for his plane.

CHAPTER TWO

LARA sat in her office overlooking the Baltimore harbor and told herself the next couple of hours were going to be a piece of cake.

She was ready. More than ready, after two weeks of preparation. She'd gone through the proposal for the new headquarters building more times than she could count. And she'd found the flaws she needed to keep Slade Baron out of Baltimore, and out of her life.

Slade Baron. How perfectly the name suited the man. Lara puffed out a breath, reached for her coffee mug and brought it to her lips. No way he'd have gone through life with a name like Brown or Smith. "Baron," with all the medieval entitlements it suggested, suited a man like that just fine.

The mug trembled in her hand. She whispered a short, sharp word and put it down before she ended up spilling coffee on her suit. The last thing she needed was to walk into that meeting feeling anything less than perfectly put together.

She'd be fine. Just fine. Of course she would. Lara stroked her hand lightly over the folder on her desk, pushed back her chair and walked to the window. She had a wonderful view from here, straight out over the harbor. A corner office, she thought, with a little smile. It had taken her six long years to work up to one but she'd done it. She had everything she'd ever wanted. A career. A title. A handsome little house in a pleasant neighborhood. And the joy of her life, the very heart of her life...

The intercom buzzed. She swung around and hit the On button.

21

"Yes, Nancy?"

"Mr. Dobbs's secretary phoned, Ms. Stevens. Mr. Baron's plane finally got in. He should be here soon."

Lara felt her stomach lurch. She touched her fingertips to her forehead, which felt as if somebody with a jackhammer had been working away at it most of the morning.

"Thank you, Nancy. Let me know when the meeting begins, please."

"Of course, Ms. Stevens."

The panic was threatening to overwhelm her. Be calm, she told herself again. She'd done what she had to do, that night eighteen months ago in Denver. Heaven knew she didn't regret it. Slade had been a means to an end, that was all. Just a means to...

His arms, hard around her. His mouth against hers. The feel of him deep within her, and the way he'd held her afterward, as if he cherished her...

Lara shuddered and wrapped her arms around herself. There was no point in thinking that way. She didn't have to romanticize what she'd done. Slade had gotten what he'd wanted and so had she, and now she had to make sure it stayed like that.

She let her gaze wander out over the water. The day was muggy, the sky filled with clouds. The weather had been very different, when she'd met Slade. Lara closed her eyes. She didn't want to remember that day...

That day in Denver.

The sky had been a dirty gray, and the snow as thick as feathers spilling from a torn pillow. Lara, trapped in the waiting area at the Denver airport, had felt impatient and irritable.

It was her thirtieth birthday, and this was one hell of a way to celebrate it.

Nothing had gone right for her that entire week, starting with not one but two baby showers for women she worked with, and ending with an ultrapolite kiss-off from Tom. Not that the relationship had gone beyond dinner and the theater but still, it wasn't pleasant, getting an earnest speech about how she was a wonderful woman, an intelligent woman...

What he'd meant was that they weren't getting anywhere. She didn't make men think about white picket fences and wedding rings. Other men had given her the same message, and she thought about that while she waited for the snow to let up.

She knew Tom was right. She had nothing against men. Maybe she was a little cool, a little distant. She'd been told that by a couple of guys. Maybe she didn't think sex was the mind-blowing experience other women did, but so what? She liked men well enough.

It was just that marriage was something else. In her heart, she knew she really didn't want to be anybody's wife. She was self-sufficient and independent, and she'd seen, first-hand, what a mess a man could make of a woman's life. Her mother, and now her sister, could have been advertisements extolling the benefits of spinsterhood.

No, marriage wasn't for her, but motherhood was. She'd known that ever since her teens, when she'd earned pocket money baby-sitting. Having babies was more than a biological need: it was a need of the heart. There was something indescribably wonderful about children. Their trust in you. Their innocence. The way they gave their love, unconditionally, and accepted yours in return.

Lara had all the love in the world to give, but her time was running out. She was thirty, and she figured she had about as much chance of having a child as an Eskimo had of getting conked on the head by a falling coconut. Thirty was far from middle-aged but there were times she felt as if she were the only woman in the world who didn't have a baby in her arms or in her belly, and that most of the women who did were years her junior.

Like the two girls she worked with. Goodness knew she wished both of them well but watching their excitement at their baby showers, she'd felt an awful emptiness because she'd suddenly known she'd never share that special joy.

She knew single women adopted babies all the time but, perhaps selfishly, Lara yearned for a child of her own. She knew about artificial insemination, too, but the thought of knowing little about the prospective father made her uneasy. She'd even considered asking someone like Tom, someone she liked and respected, to make her pregnant, but there'd been an item on the TV news about a man who'd agreed to just such an arrangement until he saw his son. All of a sudden, he'd changed his mind. Now, he was suing for joint custody.

"If I'd picked up a stranger in a bar," the girl had said, her eyes red and teary, "some guy with looks and enough brains to carry on an intelligent conversation, I'd have my baby but I wouldn't be in this mess."

Lara sat thinking all these things on that fateful afternoon in Denver, while she waited for the snow to stop.

The public address system bleated out guarded encouragement from time to time, but you didn't need a degree in meteorology to see that the storm was getting worse instead of better. After a while, she collected her computer and her carry-on, made her way to the first-class lounge, found a seat and settled in. Her mood was as foul as the weather. She took out her computer and turned it on. Solitaire was mindless; she could play it until her brain went numb.

Except that her computer wouldn't start. The battery was dead. It was the final straw, and she glared at the damned thing, contemplated hurling it to the floor, then settled for telling it what she thought of it, under her breath.

She heard a soft, masculine chuckle, and then a man's voice.

"Here you go, darling," he said.

Lara looked up. A man was standing in front of her. He was tall, he was probably what some women would call handsome, and if he thought she was in the mood for some fun and games, he was about to have his smug little smile stuffed right up his nose.

She drew herself up and looked at him as coldly as she could.

"I beg your pardon?"

But not coldly enough, apparently. His smile broadened and he shot a pointed look at the person seated in the chair next to hers. Lara lifted her brows. Obviously he was accustomed to having things his way. Well, she thought as the wimp beside her gave up his seat, this bozo was in for a big surprise.

"I am the answer to your prayers, Sugar," her unwanted visitor said. He had a drawl of some kind. Not Southern; she knew Southern drawls. Western, maybe. That would explain the lean, rangy look to him, and those ridiculous cowboy boots.

"I am not named 'Sugar,'" she said coldly. "You're out of your league, cowboy. If those boots of yours are made for walking, you'd better let them walk."

He grinned. It was, she had to admit, a nice grin on a nice face. Definitely handsome, if you liked men who looked as if they'd just ridden down from the hills, despite what had to be a hand-tailored suit and a Burberry raincoat. Not that any of that changed the fact that she wasn't interested.

"Ah," he said, "I see. You think this is just an old-fashioned pickup."

Lara gave a wide-eyed stare. "My goodness," she said sweetly, "isn't it?"

The stranger sighed, as if she'd wounded him deeply. Then he opened his computer case and took out a battery. She saw, right away, it was the duplicate of hers.

"It's painful to be misjudged, Sugar," he said. "You need a battery for your computer and I just happen to have an extra. Now, does that sound like a pickup line to you?"

Of course it did. Lara started to tell him he was wasting his time. But his eyes were twinkling, and what was the harm in admitting she saw the humor in the situation? A few minutes of conversation might make the interminable delay seem less onerous.

"Yes," she said, and smiled, to show she wasn't really offended.

"Well, you're right. But you have to admit, it's creative."

She laughed, and he laughed, and that was the way it all began.

"Hi," he said, and held out his hand. "I'm Slade."

She hesitated, then took his hand. "I'm Lara."

A tiny electric jolt passed between them.

"Static electricity," she said quickly, and pulled back her hand.

"Or something." He smiled again. "I couldn't help but overhear your, uh, your conversation. The one you were having with yourself. I didn't actually hear what you called your dead battery, but I have a pretty good imagination."

She laughed. "I'm afraid I wasn't being very polite."

"I'm serious about giving you that extra battery."

"Thanks, but I can do without it."

"Well, I'll lend it to you, then. So you can check your e-mail, or whatever."

"I did that, just before the stupid thing died. Actually it's the 'whatever' part that I was going for." She smiled. "I was going to play solitaire."

His brows lifted. They were dark brows, winged a little at the ends, and went nicely with his black, silky-looking hair. "Computer solitaire. The wonder of the age," he said with a dead-serious expression. "One card or three?"

"One, of course. Timed, with Vegas rules..."

"The deck with the palm trees?"

Lara laughed. "Uh-huh. I like that little face that appears, the one that grins when you least expect it."

"Ah, the wonders of the chip," the stranger said, and they fell into easy conversation—except she really wasn't quite sure what either of them was saying.

She thought about that electrical jolt she'd felt when she'd put her hand in his. It hadn't been static electricity at all; it had been a tingling sense of sexual awareness. She'd never felt it before but that didn't mean she was incapable of recognizing it.

And why not? This man, this stranger named Slade, was, to put it simply, gorgeous.

Tall, dark and handsome. Three little words but, when applied to him, spectacular. Coal-black hair. Smoky-gray eyes shaded by thick, black lashes. A blade of a nose set above a firm mouth and a square, dimpled chin. And even inside that custom-tailored suit, Lara could tell he had the kind of body the guys at her health club sweated for but never quite managed to achieve. He had a nice sense of humor, too, and he was intelligent...

And, just like that, the voice of the girl in the TV interview zipped through her head.

If I'd picked up a stranger in a bar, some guy with good looks and enough brains to carry on an intelligent conversation...

Lara knew she was blushing but she couldn't help it. A stranger in a bar? My God, what was wrong with her? Here he was, this hunky stranger, looking for a way to pass the time while the snow kept them trapped in the airport, and here *she* was, thinking that he'd be the right man to father her baby.

Not that there was anything wrong in thinking about it, because she'd never do such a thing. Of course not. Have sex with a stranger? Not her. But she knew how easy it would be. An exchange of business cards, the suggestion that he look her up if he came to Atlanta or even something more specific, say, a deliberate plan to meet somewhere for a weekend...

Lara let her thoughts drift. No, it wouldn't be difficult at all. He was interested in her, that was obvious. And he had a way about him that suggested he'd be good in bed, that he'd know how to bring a woman pleasure. Not that pleasure mattered, in a situation like this. It was all hypothetical, and you didn't need to enjoy sex just to get pregnant. Still, he'd know all the right moves.

She knew she was blushing again but she couldn't help it. Such wacky thoughts to be having, especially for a woman who had a sexual past uninteresting and unvaried enough to almost be embarrassing. But as long as she was indulging herself in this fantasy, there was no harm in imagining that he'd be good in bed. After all, she'd only have the one chance at getting pregnant. Weren't there statistics that showed orgasm increased those chances?

Something must have shown in her face because suddenly, in the middle of a sentence, he stopped talking and just stared at her. She was on the verge of grabbing her stuff and fleeing when he asked her if she wanted some coffee.

What she wanted was to stop thinking these insane thoughts.

Tell him no, she told herself, and then get up and walk away...

"Yes," she said, "I'd love some."

He rose from his chair. She did, too. They walked to the rear of the lounge, poured some coffee, sat down on a small sofa in a corner and she tried, really tried, to concentrate on what he was saying and to stop thinking nonsense, like how it might feel if he kissed her.

Thoughts like that had never occupied her mind before.

They did, now.

And when he refilled her cup and his hand brushed hers, she felt as if she'd been shot through with a low-voltage electrical charge. A stranger in a bar, she thought again, and she forced a little laugh.

"Whoops," she said. "One of us needs to be grounded before we go up in flames."

She knew, instantly, it was the wrong thing to say. It sounded like a come-on and she hadn't meant it like that...had she?

It was obvious what Slade thought. His eyes darkened, and a little muscle knotted just beside his mouth.

"Going up in flames might be fun," he said in a voice that sent shivers up her spine.

She felt a tremor go through her, and she began chattering inanely about something else. Anything, to lessen the growing tension. He could handle this; he was that type of man, the kind who probably left swooning women behind him wherever he went. But she couldn't. She felt as if she were letting her sanity slip away.

Silence built between them.

"You're beautiful," he said softly.

So are you, she thought, and blushed. "Thank you."

"What does your hair look like, when it's loose?"

The intimacy of the question stunned her. "What?"

"Your hair. Is it long? Does it fall over your shoulders, and your breasts?" He took the cup from her and put it on the table beside him. "This isn't just another pickup line," he said softly. "You know it's not."

She looked into his eyes and what she saw was her undoing. No man had ever looked at her this way, had ever made her feel this way. Desirable. Sexy. Seductive. She knew what he was thinking, that he was imagining what it would be like to undress her, take down her hair, kiss her and stroke her and make her sob out his name...

An announcement blared over the loudspeaker. Thank God, Lara thought, and focused her attention on the disembodied voice.

All flights were grounded until further notice. The airline would try to make arrangements for overnight accommodations for passengers who wanted them.

Lara cleared her throat. "Well," she said, and gave a forced laugh, "well, that's that."

Slade nodded, and she was sure he understood what she meant. "Yes." He smiled politely. "Are you going to wait it out here?"

"Uh-huh. How about you?"

"Yes," he said, and then, so quickly that she wasn't sure

it had happened, his eyes went from smoky-gray to deepest charcoal. "The hell with this," he said. "Come with me."

Lara didn't pretend not to understand. "No," she whispered, "I can't."

"Are you married?" She shook her head. "Engaged?" She shook her head again. Slade moved closer, until she could feel the warmth of his breath on her face. "Neither am I. We won't be hurting anyone." He reached out and took her hand. She let him do it, though she knew it was a mistake. "Come to bed with me, Lara."

There it was, out in the open. What he'd been thinking, what she'd been thinking. And here was her chance. But she wouldn't take it. Sleep with a strange man, deliberately try to get herself pregnant without his knowledge...

"No." She shook her head and said the words again. "I can't."

"We'll be incredible together," he said in a husky whisper.

"I couldn't," she stammered. "I—I don't even know you."

"Yes, you do. You've known me forever, the same as I've known you." His voice was rough and low. "As for the details... I'm an architect. I live in Boston. I'm straight, I'm not married, not committed to anyone. I'm twenty-eight years old, I just had my annual physical and my doctor says I'm healthy enough to outlive Methuselah. And I've never wanted a woman the way I want you."

Lara looked at him. She felt as if she'd stepped into another dimension, a dimension in which anything was possible and everything was acceptable. Who would she hurt, if she went with him? He wanted her. She wanted a child.

No. No, it was worse than crazy, it was immoral. Wasn't it?

She swallowed dryly, then licked her lips.

"It's—it's crazy. Even talking like this—"

He put his finger lightly across her mouth. She shuddered

at the feel of it on her skin. A lazy lick of flame began curling through her blood. Oh, it would be so easy...

"I'll get a taxi," he murmured. "There's a hotel not far from here. They know me. They'll find us a room."

"A taxi. And a hotel, in weather like this?" She made a sound that she hoped was a laugh. "You're very sure of yourself, Slade."

"If I were sure of myself," he said softly, "I wouldn't be holding my breath while I wait for your answer."

She looked up at him, and thought of what it would be like to go with him. To have him touch her. Not just because she wanted a child but—*be honest, Lara*—but because he was the most exciting man she'd ever met, because she was dizzy with wanting to be in his arms...

"Lara?"

She took a deep, deep breath. And she said, "Yes."

He took her to the hotel. His arm lay heavy around her waist, anchoring her to him as if he thought she'd change her mind and run away. He started to stop at the shop in the lobby and she knew it was so he could buy condoms.

She took an even deeper breath and told him it wasn't necessary.

He didn't question her, but the press of his hand at her waist grew more possessive as he led her to their room.

She didn't panic until he shut the door and locked it. When he turned toward her, she looked at him and saw a stranger.

What am I doing? she thought frantically. Her heart thumped with fear.

"No!" she said, "no, I can't do this."

Perhaps if he'd tried to talk her into it, or if he'd pulled her into his arms, things would have ended differently. But he did neither of those things. He took her face in his hands, his touch sure and gentle. And he kissed her so tenderly that it made her feel breathless.

His mouth was wonderful, soft and warm on hers. She felt the fear slipping from her body, felt something hot and exciting take its place. She wrapped her hands around his wrists and, slowly, the kiss changed, grew hungry and demanding, and she moaned and looped her arms around his neck.

Now, she thought, now, before I lose courage…

"Please," she whispered, "oh, Slade, please."

And he carried her to the bed, undressed her, let down her hair and fulfilled every middle-of-the night dream she'd ever had, and some she'd never dared imagine.

The storm became a blizzard. Lara didn't care. She never left Slade's arms, never wanted to. She forgot the reason she'd come with him and remembered only that he was the lover she'd always longed for.

He was everything, the perfect fantasy, and yet he was real.

She fell asleep at last, exhausted, her head on his chest, and awakened to his kisses at dawn. She looked up at him and knew she'd been a fool to think she wanted him only so he could give her a baby. She still wanted that but now she wanted more.

She wanted Slade, in her arms and in her life. And, if the past hours meant anything, she thought he might want that, too. In fact, there was a darkness in his eyes that she suspected came of the realization that the long, wonderful night was going to end.

She smiled, to let him know she didn't want it to happen, either. "Slade? What's wrong?"

"Nothing. I mean, the storm's over." He smiled, and her heart plummeted because suddenly she knew she'd misunderstood what she'd seen in his eyes. It wasn't fear that the night would end, it was panic that she might want more than he wanted to give. "Lara, this was wonderful. Maybe—maybe we can manage to get together again sometime."

She felt the sting of tears in her eyes and hated herself for it. She reminded herself that he'd made her no promises, that she'd wanted no promises, and she smiled and assured him that would be great. She had the awful feeling he was going to apologize for having hurt her feelings and she stopped him by reaching for him, touching him, and making him forget everything but the need to possess her again.

When it was done, he made an attempt at sincerity.

"I don't know your address," he said. "Or your phone number."

"I'll give them to you in the morning," Lara had answered, but she'd known she was lying. She'd waited until he fell asleep. Then she'd dressed and let herself quietly from the room.

She hadn't gone with him for passion, she'd gone for what he could give her. For a child. That was all she'd wanted from him...

Wasn't it? she thought, as she stared out at the Baltimore harbor.

Lara swung away from the window. Her intercom was buzzing. She cleared her throat and reached for it.

"Ms. Stevens? Mr. Baron's arrived. He's in the conference room, with the directors. Mr. Dobbs says would you please join them now?"

"Thank you, Nancy."

She sounded calm. That was good. She looked it, too, she thought as she took out her compact and peered into it. But her hand trembled a little as she smoothed back her hair.

"Don't be an idiot, Lara," she told her reflection. She was prepared. She knew what she had to do and how to do it. She'd get Slade Baron out of Baltimore so quickly it would make his head spin. As for facing him—that wasn't a problem. What she'd felt for him, what she'd thought she felt, had never been real.

Lara smoothed down her skirt, plucked the folder from her desk and left her office.

CHAPTER THREE

LARA swiped the palms of her hands against her skirt as she rode the elevator to the conference room level.

Stop it, she told herself angrily. The advantage was hers. Slade wouldn't be expecting to see her. He hadn't known her last name, any more than she'd known his. He was going to be the one who would have to work at showing no reaction to the discovery that Beaufort's chief auditor was the woman he'd slept with on a snowy night in Denver.

She had to calm down, otherwise she'd not only lose that advantage, she'd never be able to carry this off. Slade would see her panic and he, smug male animal that he was, would take it as a sign that she was overcome with excitement at seeing him again.

Overcome, yes. But not with excitement. With fear. And there was nothing to fear. Nothing.

The elevator door slid open. Lara took a breath, squared her shoulders and strode down the hall.

"They're waiting for you," Dobbs's secretary chirped.

Lara took her chances and tried a smile. "Thanks."

It worked. The secretary didn't leap to her feet and run, screaming, to the elevator, which, Lara supposed, meant she really was smiling and not just pulling her lips back from her teeth like a rabid dog baring its fangs. But that was certainly how it felt.

The massive doors to the conference room stood open. Lara's heart thudded. She hesitated in the doorway while she scanned the room for Slade. Where was he? The room was big. Huge, really. Six months ago, when she'd transferred from the Atlanta office to this one, she'd attended a meeting in it and been amazed at the room's enormity.

There he was, standing at the windows with his back to her. It didn't matter that she couldn't see his face. She knew him just the same. His height. The width of his shoulders. That midnight-black hair. And the way he stood, with a sort of sexy, king of the universe arrogance.

It was Slade, just as she remembered him. Slade, the fantasy-lover whose arms had held her all through that long-ago night. Whose arms still held her in the dreams she acknowledged only in the darkness before dawn…

Slade, whose long, lean body suddenly stiffened.

She held her breath, told herself it was impossible he'd sensed her presence but even as she gave herself all those reassurances, she knew. She felt like a trapped animal as he turned toward her.

A dozen reactions raced across his handsome face. Surprise. Shock. Then a slow, sexy smile of delight.

Oh, God.

The room spun; her vision narrowed but she stood her ground, looked at him coolly and then looked away. He wasn't going to seduce her again. Not this time, not even into complacency. The sooner he understood that, the better.

"Ah, there you are, Ms. Stevens."

Lara tilted her chin and turned away, toward Edwin Dobbs.

"Mr. Dobbs," she said pleasantly. "I hope I haven't kept you waiting."

"No, no. You're right on time." Dobbs took her arm and moved her forward, and a good thing he did, Lara thought, because it felt as if she were walking on a carpet made of marshmallow. "I believe you know all the members of the board."

"Certainly. How do you do, Mr. Rogers? Nice to see you again, Mr. Kraemer."

She smiled. She shook hands. Answered yes, the weather was unusually cool, participated in the mindless chitchat the directors undoubtedly thought would make them seem like regular fellows.

Inside herself, she trembled.

She'd caught Slade off balance—that look on his face, before he'd realized he had no effect on her anymore, had said it all. The trouble was, for one heart-wrenching moment, she'd wanted to smile back, to run across the room and into his arms.

"...our new architect, Mr. Slade Baron."

Lara's heart banged into her throat. Dobbs had led her across the room, to Slade. And Slade had stopped smiling. He was looking at her as if he'd moved a rock and uncovered a new species of life.

"Mr. Baron," she said politely, and held out her hand.

"Such formality, Lara," Slade said, just as politely, and clasped her fingers in his.

Dobbs's eyebrows rose. "Do you two know each other?"

"No," Lara said.

"Yes," Slade said, at the same instant, and laughed. "I suspect what Lara means is that we don't actually know each other very well. Isn't that right, Lara?"

Lara looked up at him. He was smiling now, but there was a tiny muscle dancing at the corner of his mouth, and his eyes were as gray as a storm-tossed sea.

"Yes," she said stupidly, because Slade had taken command of the game. All she could do was follow where he led and hope to hell she could get out in one piece. "We, uh, we don't know each other very well," she parroted, and pulled her hand from his.

Dobbs nodded thoughtfully. "Isn't that interesting? Ms. Stevens, you never said a word about knowing Mr. Baron."

"No. Ah, no, I didn't. You see—you see—"

"Well, she couldn't." Slade flashed a lazy grin. "Considering that we never did get around to exchanging last names."

Oh please, Lara thought, please, let the ground open up and swallow me.

"We met at an airport, oh, a year and a half or so ago,

and ended up spending a bit of time together. Isn't that right, Lara?"

"The weather," she said jerkily. "It was—"

"Snowing. My oh my, it surely was." Slade laughed politely. "I don't think I ever saw that much snow before, Mr. Dobbs. But your Ms. Stevens is a clever lady. Between us, we found lots of ways to pass the time."

"Did you, now?" Dobbs said, with a puzzled smile.

"Oh, yes. We... But I'll let her tell you all about it."

Dobbs looked at Lara. Lara licked her lips. "I—I can't imagine you'd be interested in—in the details, sir."

"Of course he is," Slade said.

"Of course I am," Dobbs echoed, his brows still lifted.

"There I was," Slade said, "trying to figure out how I could possibly make the time do anything but crawl." He looked at Lara, the smile still on his face but his eyes as flat and cold as ice. "And then, fortunately for me, your Ms. Stevens and I struck up a conversation."

"About nothing," Lara said, with a tight little laugh. "You know how it is, Mr. Dobbs, two strangers just—just dealing in a lot of small talk, to pass the time."

"But," Slade said lazily, "as it turned out, we had a lot in common. Ms. Stevens's battery needed charging. And mine just happened to be fully charged."

Lara could feel her face burning. "Computers," she said wildly. "That's what he's talking about. We both use the same kind. And my battery died. And he said I could borrow his. And—and..."

She fell silent. Slade was smiling. It was the most polite smile Lara had ever seen but there was nothing polite in what he was really saying. She could read the subtext. A woman wasn't supposed to sneak out of a man's bed the way she had, even if she was just a one-night stand. And she certainly wasn't supposed to turn up in his life again, especially not in a business setting.

His ego was on the line—but so was everything that

meant anything to her. The realization gave her the courage she needed.

"Anyway," she said, and flashed a brilliant smile, "Mr. Baron was kind enough to offer his services." She turned the thousand-watt smile on Slade and saw, with a thrill of pleasure, that he hadn't expected such a quick recovery. "I must admit," she said briskly, "I'd forgotten all about your generosity. How nice to see you again, and to be reminded of it."

"Well," Edwin Dobbs said, and cleared his throat, "now that we've made all the introductions... Mr. Baron? Would you like to begin your presentation?"

"Of course," Slade said, and wondered if anybody but Lara knew he was lying through his teeth.

He'd done this a thousand times, so it required no thought. Open his computer, turn it on, use a projector to bring up screen after screen of dazzling design and detail, pointing out all the elements while the board members followed along, entranced.

And a damn good thing he had done it a thousand times, Slade thought grimly, or he'd be standing here like a fool, steam coming out of his ears and nonsense coming out of his mouth.

"Our auditor has been going through your proposal," Dobbs had told him, before the start of the meeting. "I've asked her to join us so we can be sure we agree on the projected costs of your design, Mr. Baron."

"No problem," Slade had said politely.

Just then, he'd gotten a strange, prickling sensation along his spine. Someone was looking at him, he'd thought, and he'd turned to see her in the doorway. Lara. The woman he couldn't get out of his head, and he'd thought how incredible it was that he'd found her again.

Every cliché about it being a small world had tripped through his mind. He'd felt the smile begin spreading across his face as he waited for her to see him—but when she did, the coldness in her eyes tumbled him straight back to reality.

She'd known he'd be here.

Of course she'd known. Dobbs had given her his proposal. She had the file under her arm, and Slade knew what was in it. All the design data. And all his personal data. His name. His phone number. His address.

And, just in case there was any doubt, his photo.

Lara had known who he was, that she'd be seeing him today, and she'd kept that knowledge to herself. No phone call. No e-mail. No letter saying, Slade, guess what…?

She'd deliberately let him walk into this setup, as if he were an enemy. Not only hadn't she wanted to see him again, but she'd deliberately set things up so he'd walk in here and—

And what?

He still had no idea.

What had he stumbled into? It was shock enough to see her after all this time and to realize he'd be working with her, but why was she so icy? He wasn't the one who'd slunk out of that bedroom.

"…can see that I've incorporated your wish to maintain tradition with an awareness of the forward-looking principles of the future…"

Was he still making sense? Evidently. The directors' attention was still fixed on him.

But not Lara's.

She sat next to Edwin Dobbs, her hands folded neatly on the polished surface of the conference-room table. Their eyes met, and a coldness swept through Slade's blood. She was watching him as if he were standing at his own gravesite with a shovel in his hand.

"…a reflecting pool, here, in the atrium garden…"

Her face was a perfect blank.

What in *hell* was going on here?

He flashed back, again, to that moment he'd first seen her in the doorway. The shock of it had smashed into him like a hot poker and, yeah, the pleasure, too. There'd been other women in his life since that night, sure, but the thing was, there'd been nobody quite like her.

And he'd thought, I'll tell her that, after this meeting ends, I'll say, Look, now that fate brought us together again, what are you doing this weekend?

Until he saw her looking at him as if she were a cat and he was a portion of breast of sparrow. He didn't like it, not one bit. This was the woman who was going to advise the Beaufort bank directors on the reliability of his figures?

It wasn't going to happen.

He wanted to tell her that, to say, I see that look in your eyes, Sugar, and believe me, you are the very last person on the planet I'd ever trust. You might be a firecracker in bed but...

Man, she surely was.

He could remember the heat of her, in his arms. The little tricks she knew that almost had him thinking she was sweet and innocent, that she'd never done anything like shacking up with a stranger before. Those little moans of hers, and the way she'd touched him at first, kind of shy and questioning...

Hell.

Slade caught himself, frowned and took a quick look around the conference table. He half expected to see Dobbs and the others staring at him as if he'd lost his mind but they were all intent on the pictures on the screen.

Thank God for small favors.

His libido might have been in a Denver hotel room but the part of his brain that mattered was on automatic pilot. He'd finished his presentation and it had gone well. He could tell by the pleased expression on Dobbs's face, and by the little buzz around the table.

Lara's face was still a polite mask.

"Thank you very much, Mr. Baron," Dobbs said. "That was most illuminating."

Might as well cut straight to the chase, Slade thought, and looked at Lara.

"I'm glad to hear it," he said. "But Ms. Stevens looks as if she has some questions."

"Yes," Lara said, "in fact, I do."

She didn't just have questions, she had statements and speeches, and pages of mind-bending figures. Slade had read her right. She had an agenda all her own. She wanted him out of here, and she'd do anything to accomplish it.

Within minutes, the conference table was buried under piles of paper. Articles. Clippings. Printouts. She had documentation that probably went straight back to the design of the Pyramids, all of it detailing the financial disasters that could befall a project between its plan and its completion. She had more stuff in her briefcase than he had in his office back in Boston, and she distributed it with the gusto of a clerk handing out free cereal samples in a supermarket.

Slade could smell the stink of doubt oozing into the air. Furrows appeared in the foreheads of the men who'd been beaming at him only moments before. And, in the midst of it all, Lara looked up, caught his eye and gave him a tight, condescending smile.

He smiled right back.

It was either that, or kill her.

What was with this woman? Wasn't it enough that she'd left him high and dry in that hotel room? Did she need to make him look like a jerk here, too?

He could see himself vaulting the table, grabbing her and shaking her until her teeth rattled...or, better still, backing her against the wall, thrusting his hands into that silky mass of hair until it tumbled down over her shoulders, kissing that irritating little smile off her mouth. He could almost feel the smoothness of her jacket, the silkiness of her blouse and then the hot satin of her flesh as her breasts filled his hands.

That would tell her that she might be able to fool these idiots but she couldn't fool him, couldn't sit there and pretend that memories of that night hadn't stayed with her. Was that her problem? Did she think running him out of town would eliminate those images? Or was this payback for that little speech he'd made about hoping they'd bump into each other again, sometime?

Either way, she'd made a mistake. If this was a battlefield, he was prepared to fight.

He waited patiently while she spoke, keeping his expression neutral, his hands in his pockets so nobody would see he'd knotted them into fists. Eventually she ran out of numbers, and she looked at Dobbs.

"I'm sorry to have to make all these negative comments, sir," she said, with what Slade knew the others would accept as genuine regret. "Mr. Baron's design is excellent, I'm sure. I just don't see that Beaufort can go ahead with this project within the defined budgetary constraints." She looked at Slade. "Unless," she said politely, "I've missed something...?"

Her smile, her voice, made it clear such a thing was impossible.

The room was silent. Dobbs and the other men looked from Lara to Slade.

"Well, Mr. Baron," the chairman said, after clearing his throat, "I'm sure you have some comment to offer."

Slade nodded. "Yes," he said evenly, "I do."

He walked across the room, knowing every eye was on him, stalling a little to make sure he regained his composure. When he reached the windows, he took a deep breath and turned around. The men were watching him with interest but the look on Lara's face had gone from smug anticipation to wary concern.

"My compliments, Ms. Stevens. That was quite an interesting presentation." He flashed a quick smile around the table, one that made it clear he'd have offered similar praise to a precocious three-year-old who'd managed to get all the way through her *ABC*s. Slade looked at Dobbs and his smile faded. "Interesting—but inaccurate. Ms. Stevens seems to be confused on several key points."

It took him less than five minutes to refute her arguments,

actually, to reduce them to rubble. In Lara's zeal to run him out of town—and Slade was sure that had been her intention—she'd made mistakes. She knew lots about numbers but nothing about architecture. And she sure as hell had underestimated him as an adversary.

When he'd finished, the room was silent. After a moment, Dobbs looked around, engaged the others in some kind of unspoken communication, then put his hands, palms flattened, on the table.

"Well, Mr. Baron, it's obvious you've done your homework."

Slade smiled pleasantly. "I always do," he said, and thought that this was probably the first time in his life he'd come up with anything positive he could attribute to his old man, who'd done what he could to beat that philosophy into the seat of his pants.

"Wantin' ain't enough, boy," Jonas would say. "You got to go in prepared to win."

Well, he'd wanted to win this commission. And he'd come prepared, not for a personal attack, which this damned well was, but for the usual nit-picking of bean counters. It was just that he'd never expected the bean-counter to be a blue-eyed, strawberry-blonde named Lara.

It made the victory he knew was his all the sweeter. He'd have stood on his head, if that's what it took, to teach her that she couldn't make a fool of Slade Baron a second time. Because, dammit, she *had* made a fool of him, sneaking out of his bed that way, and it was time he admitted it.

Dobbs pushed back his chair and stood, an obvious signal that the meeting was over. Everyone else rose, too, including Lara.

"Thank you for your input, Ms. Stevens. You certainly raised some important issues and the board will take them under advisement."

Lara nodded stiffly. "You're welcome, sir."

Dobbs came around the table and clapped Slade on the

back. "I hope you don't think our Ms. Stevens gave you too difficult a time."

"No, not at all." He looked at Lara. Her face was expressionless as, he hoped, was his. He still couldn't figure out why she'd tried to sabotage him. None of the reasons he'd come up with really made sense...unless she was involved with some other guy.

Slade's jaw tightened.

Yeah, that would explain it. She was seeing somebody else and suddenly, here he was, walking, talking proof of the fact that she'd once spent a hot night with a strange man.

He looked at her left hand, and saw a thin gold band on her ring finger.

Years before, when he was a kid, a bronc had bucked him off. He'd hit his head, hard. All Slade could ever recall of the incident was going down into a spinning whirlpool of darkness. That was the way he felt now.

Married. Lara was married.

He tore his eyes from her hand, dragged air into his lungs. Okay, she was married. So what? It was nothing to him. What they'd shared had been sex, that was all, and it had happened a long time ago. She'd gone her way, he'd gone his, and now she had a husband.

At least that explained things, though she flattered herself if she thought he'd want her again, want her badly enough to threaten to tell her husband about them. But there was no "them." There never had been and besides, the day he had to coerce a woman into bed was the day he'd check himself into a retirement home.

It just plain infuriated him that she'd thought she needed to protect herself by screwing him over. He wanted to tell her that—but she'd already packed up her things and left.

Running out seemed to be Lara's thing. Well, she wasn't going to get away with it this time.

Slade shook hands all around. Dobbs walked him to the door.

"We'll be in touch soon, Mr. Baron."

Slade nodded. "That's fine. Oh, by the way…your Ms. Stevens made some references to purchasing procedures that were inaccurate."

"A diligent young woman, Ms. Stevens." Dobbs chuckled. "Just between us, I'm afraid she went a bit overboard."

"Diligent, as you said, sir. But I'd like to correct her about those procedures. Would you know where I might find her?"

"In Finance. Fourth floor. The receptionist there can direct you. Nice of you to want to help straighten her out, Mr. Baron—or may I call you Slade?"

"You may, indeed," Slade replied, and smiled. "And believe me, Edwin, straightening out Lara Stevens will be a pleasure."

The receptionist was obliging, and pointed him in the right direction.

Lara's secretary was not. "You can't go in there unannounced," she said, and leaped to her feet, but Slade had already turned the knob and flung open the door.

Lara was standing at the window. She swung around at the sound of the intrusion, the color draining from her face when she saw Slade.

"Ms. Stevens, I tried to tell this gentleman that he couldn't just barge his way into your office—"

"Tell your secretary to go away," Slade said coldly.

"Ms. Stevens, if you'd like me to call security…?"

Slade moved into the room. "Tell her, dammit."

Lara swallowed. "It's all right, Nancy." Her voice was steady and calm. It surprised her, because her pulse was going crazy. She couldn't let him make a scene. "Really," she said brightly, "it's fine. This is Mr. Baron. We, ah, we had some disagreements during the meeting just now…" Lara pasted a smile to her lips. "That will be all, Nancy. Thank you."

Slade waited until he heard the door close behind him.

"I underestimated you, Sugar," he said softly.

"What do you want, Slade?"

He dumped his things in a chair and strolled toward her. "Here I'd ticketed you for bein' nothin' more substantial than a hot babe lookin' for a good time..."

Her face was still white as paper but she didn't move a muscle.

"...lookin' for a good time and now it turns out you've got all the instincts of a shark."

Lara stepped forward and folded her arms. This was her turf, not his, and she'd be damned if she'd let him intimidate her. "I'm asking you again, Slade. What do you want?"

"Just the chance to congratulate you." He smiled lazily. "You put on one hell of a fine performance for the boys in the boardroom, Ms. Stevens." He paused, just long enough to make it count. "Or should that be *Mrs.?*"

"Mrs...." She caught her bottom lip between her teeth, looked down at the thin band of gold on her ring finger, then at him. "Yes."

"That's it? Just, 'yes'?" Slade leaned a hip against the edge of her desk. "Come on, Sugar. You can do better than that. When did you get hitched? Since we last met?" This time, his smile was all teeth. "Or did you maybe just 'forget' to wear your ring when we had our little, ah, encounter?"

That got to her. Her shoulders squared and the look she shot him was filled with loathing.

"I won't even dignify that comment with an answer. Now, if you'll excuse me—"

"Who's the lucky guy? I might just give him a call, invite him for a couple of beers."

She thought of inventing a name, then thought better of it. "I know it will break your heart to hear this but you won't have the chance. I'm divorced."

Slade's brows arched. "Is that a fact? Married and divorced, all in a year and a half. My oh my, darlin'. You've certainly been busy."

Lara pulled back her chair and sat down behind her desk. "I'm really very busy. If there's a point to this visit—"

"You're damned right, there's a point." He watched her, his blood pressure easing into the red zone as she yanked a stack of papers toward her and began leafing through them. Okay, so he'd thrown her for a couple of minutes but she was in control again, acting as if he were of no more importance than a speck on the wall. "Dammit," he snarled, and shot to his feet. "You look at me when I'm talking to you, Mrs. Stevens!"

Lara raised her head. Her blue eyes were hot with defiance.

"You get out of my office, Mr. Baron!"

"I will, as soon as you've explained yourself."

"There's nothing to explain."

"There certainly is. I want to know why you ran out on me that night."

It wasn't what he'd intended to say. He'd meant to demand she tell him why she'd set him up for failure with Dobbs, why she was so eager to see the last of him, but as he said the words, he knew they were the truth.

"I don't owe you an explanation, or anything else!"

He looked down at her. Her eyes were bright, almost feverish. Her mouth trembled, and he remembered how soft it had been, under his. He told himself to turn around and walk, to get out now instead of making an ass of himself...

Oh, hell, he thought, and before she had time to move or he had time to think, he came around the desk, took hold of her and pulled her to her feet.

"Yeah," he said roughly, "you do."

And he caught her in his arms, and kissed her.

CHAPTER FOUR

How could a man be dumb enough to compound one problem with another?

Slade still hadn't come up with an answer, even though it was Monday morning and he was back home in Boston.

First he'd seduced a woman he'd met during a snowstorm. Not a mistake in itself, he thought, frowning at his image in the mirror over the bathroom sink. It was getting her stuck in his head for the past eighteen months that had not been clever.

He worked up a soapy lather in his shaving cup, then spread it over his dark stubbled jaw.

But he'd pretty much topped that by losing his cool in the Beaufort conference room. Well, not entirely. He hadn't really lost his composure; he'd just come damned close. His frown deepened as he picked up the old-fashioned straight razor he favored, honed it on its leather strop, leaned over the basin and scraped it down his cheek.

Another couple of clever double entendres, and even old man Dobbs would have figured out that something more than computer-talk had been going on between his number one financial honcho and the guy who was going to design the new Beaufort headquarters.

Slade turned on the water, rinsed the blade and angled it against his other cheek.

But none of that held a candle to that final bit of lunacy. Charging down to Lara's office. Doing a number on her secretary that probably had the woman convinced he was a certifiable psycho. Confronting Lara over what was, when you came down to it, a non-issue. Two non-issues, in fact. One, that she'd set him up, in hopes he'd stumble during

48

the meeting. Two, that she'd sneaked out of that hotel room...

That she'd left his bed, long before he'd been ready to have her leave. He'd wanted one more hour of holding her. Of kissing her...

The blade slipped. "Dammit," he snarled, as a bright drop of crimson welled on his chin.

He dumped the razor into the sink, reached down beside the commode and grabbed for a piece of tissue. What was he doing, wasting time brooding over this thing? Okay, so he'd overreacted on Friday. So what? It had been anger driving him, not passion. Lara's phone had rung, jolting him back to reality, and he'd made a quick recovery, putting her from him, turning on his heel and marching out of her office...

But not before he could have sworn he'd felt her mouth softening under his.

Blood soaked through the blob of tissue. He pulled it off, yanked open one drawer after another in the vanity under the sink until he found what remained of a styptic pencil. He scraped the point over the cut, waited for the bleeding to stop, then went into his bedroom to get dressed.

So what? The woman was nothing but trouble with a capital *T.* He'd gone to Baltimore to win a commission, and he had. By the time he got home, there was a message from Dobbs on his answering machine, telling him the job was his.

What more could a man ask?

Slade's mouth thinned.

He could ask that Lara Stevens get out of his head and leave him alone.

"Dammit," he snarled again, and instead of putting on a suit, a white-on-white shirt and a silk tie, he thumbed off his trousers, stepped into his shorts and his running shoes, yanked an ancient Harvard T-shirt over his head and trotted down the stairs, out the door and to the path along the Charles River.

He'd run it once this morning already, but he needed to run it again.

Within minutes, his T-shirt was plastered to his skin. It had been cooler, an hour ago, when he'd done his daily five-mile stint. That was okay. It was fine. Maybe running until he collapsed in a sodden heap would exorcise Lara's ghost. He was tired of having her image burned into his brain.

He could see her face, hear her voice. He could feel the heat of her, in his arms. He could almost taste her, and all three nights since he'd last kissed her, he'd awakened with the sheets kicked off and the male part of his anatomy threatening to do embarrassing things it hadn't done since he was fifteen.

Slade felt his lungs start to burn as the distance lengthened. Friday night had gone by, and Saturday, and Sunday. Plenty of time to have put Lara out of his mind.

Except, he hadn't. And he'd tried.

He'd worked all day Saturday, phoned a knockout blonde at the last minute and smiled to himself when she'd said well, she already had plans...but yes, she'd change them. So he'd taken the blonde to dinner, then to an outdoor concert. And he'd ended up in her apartment overlooking the Green, as he'd known he would—except, when she'd slipped into his arms and started undoing his tie, he'd suddenly wanted to be anyplace but where he was.

"Wow," he'd said, gently disengaging from her embrace. "I just remembered that I have to, uh, I have to go to my office."

"At midnight?" she'd said, and he'd said, yeah, right, at midnight...

And he'd fled.

Slade groaned at the memory and pumped his arms and legs faster.

He'd tried again on Sunday by almost killing himself with exercise. He'd run in the morning, danced around with the body bag at his gym for an hour after that, sculled up the river in midafternoon. In the evening, he sent out for pizza and vegged out in front of the TV.

So much for thinking about Lara, he'd thought smugly—until someplace around dawn, when he'd had one of those dreams he didn't even want to think about. And yeah, now he was running his butt off, panting and sweating as he headed home, thinking about nothing and nobody but her.

Slade stumbled up the front steps into his house and dragged himself into the shower without even taking off his soaked shorts or T-shirt. He turned his face up to the water and—he was still thinking about her, still wondering why he'd kissed her, and what would have happened if that phone hadn't rung because, no matter what she said, she still wanted to pick up where they'd left off. He'd felt her turn boneless in his arms. He'd heard that sexy little moan, felt the kick of her heart…

What kind of man would marry a woman like that and divorce her, all in a year and a half's time?

Why should it matter a damn to him? That was a better question.

"It doesn't," he said firmly, as he stepped from the shower.

Maybe it was time to take a break from the playing fields for a while. He had the Beaufort building to work on and another proposal coming up, lots of designs and meetings to deal with. In fact, he'd already penciled-in a meeting with Dobbs two weeks from now.

"Come for the whole weekend," Dobbs had said, "and I'll introduce you around, at my club."

It didn't matter that he'd have to spend two days in the same city as Lara. Thinking about her was a thing of the past, right?

"Right," Slade said.

He finished dressing, pulled on his boots, knotted his tie and made his way briskly down the stairs.

By nine, he was seated behind his desk, leafing through his calendar. He had a luncheon appointment, a conference call at three…and a memo in his own handwriting, to phone Travis.

He grinned.

Trav had been roped into some kind of bachelor auction the other night. His office had put a heavy wager on his being the bachelor who'd bring in the highest bid.

Well, why not? Trav had tried settling down and discovered it didn't work. Big surprise, Slade through wryly. The only guy he knew who'd ever settled down and been happy with one woman was Gage but then, Natalie wasn't a woman, she was an angel.

Slade put his feet up, crossed them at the ankles and linked his hands behind his head.

Playing the field was what he enjoyed, too. That, and seeing to it that Baron, Haggerty and Levine kept right on growing.

"We'll do the names in alphabetical order," he'd said the night he, Jack and Ted had hatched their plans over good pasta and bad Chianti at the little Italian *trattoria* two blocks from the offices of the giant architectural firm that had hired all three of them straight out of Harvard.

"I'll bet we wouldn't, if your name was Zambroski," Jack had said, deadpan, "but it's okay. Each time I think of you charming your way through all those Back Bay debs, Baron, I swear I can hear cash registers ringing."

Slade grinned at the memory. The truth was, he'd have lived with his name coming in last. What he couldn't have endured was if their new alliance had done the same thing. Making it mattered. He was a good architect, a damned good architect, despite his old man's reaction to his youngest son's career goals.

"You want to spend your life drawin' pictures of houses for other people," Jonas had drawled, "you go right ahead and do it. Jes' don't look to me to finance those pansy dreams, boy."

It wasn't a disappointment, it was just what Slade had expected.

"That's fine, Father," he'd said. "I'd rather do it on my own."

His high school grades stunk, no surprise considering he'd spent most of the years between sixteen and eighteen riding motorcycles, horses and women. The Baron name and hopes of a fat endowment were probably the only things that had gotten him into a small Texas college. Once there, Slade had worked his tail off to make all As and Phi Beta Kappa. That had been enough to get him into Harvard Grad School, where he'd supported himself tending bar at an off-campus pub in the financial district.

The job had changed everything. He'd picked up market savvy from stockbrokers tossing back double scotches, opened an account and placed his Dow Jones bets with the same recklessness he'd once shown for women, bikes and broncs. By the time he had his degree, he also had enough money in the bank to impress even him. A year later, he'd dumped every penny of it into the brand-new firm of Baron, Haggerty and Levine.

And B, H and L was a success.

Slade smiled. A huge success. Office buildings that transformed skylines were his specialty. Ted had become an authority on period reconstructions, and Jack was a genius at designing residences for clients who wanted something exceptional and weren't afraid to pay for it.

Life was good. Slade loved his work, his city and the life he led. He drove a dark green Jag and a shiny black Blazer. He had a cabin in the Maine woods and a Greek Revival bowfront house in Boston that he was restoring with his own hands, and just as Jack had predicted, he was doing fine—well, better than fine—with the Back Bay ladies. With the ones from Beacon Hill and Cambridge and—why be modest?—from all points of the compass. Slade smiled. Getting on with women had never been a problem.

Until now.

His smile twisted.

Until he'd had the misfortune to get involved with a woman who'd seemed as easy to read as any female he'd ever known and had, instead, turned out to be more complicated than the narrow streets that zigzagged their way through Beacon Hill.

"Mr. Baron?"

Slade looked up. His own secretary was out on maternity leave. The temp was a sweet, competent young woman but she blushed whenever she looked at him. Sometimes he thought about telling her, straight out, that she had nothing to worry about, that he never fooled around with women who worked for him or with him...

Then, what had he been doing with Lara? Kissing her, in her office. In her office!

He sat up straight and cleared his throat.

"Yes, Betsy?"

"This package just arrived, sir. By private messenger."

Slade thanked her and took it. Interesting. No name. No return address.

"Is there anything else, Mr. Baron?"

"No. Uh, yeah. Some coffee, please. Black, one sugar."

He opened the package as the door swung shut. There was a small vellum envelope inside. He took it out, sniffed it for perfume, then opened it and took out an elegant, handscripted notecard.

Your presence is requested at
The eighty-fifth birthday celebration
Of Mr. Jonas Baron
Saturday and Sunday, June the 14 and 15
At the Baron Ranch
"Espada"
Brazos Springs, Texas
RSVP

"Oh, hell," Slade muttered, and rolled his eyes not just at the invitation but at the note scrawled under the RSVP.

"No excuses," it read. "The female population of Boston will just have to do without you for one weekend." The words were emphasized by a bold capital *C*, and softened by the drawing of a tiny heart.

He couldn't help laughing. The note was from his step-sister, Caitlin, who'd figured out years ago that the only way to handle her stepbrothers was to be every bit as tough as they were. Not that it was going to get her anywhere, this time.

An eighty-fifth birthday party for the old man? Yeah, it was a shocker. Not the party; Catie, sweetheart that she was, would surely want to do something nice to celebrate the event. It was the fact that Jonas was so old that caught him by surprise. Last time he'd seen him, a couple of years ago, his father had looked as tough and hard and lean as ever. He was ageless—except, he wasn't. The invitation proved that. Still, Slade's decision was definite. He wasn't going to the party. No way. His life was crazy enough lately, without adding a weekend with dear old Dad to the mix.

Slade glanced at the clock. He had the feeling he wasn't the only one looking at a birthday party invitation just about now...

His private phone rang, just as he reached for it.

"Slade, my man," Travis drawled, "how you doin'?"

Slade smiled, picked up the vellum card and tilted back his chair.

"Well," he said, in that same Texas drawl, "I was doin' fine—until a messenger turned up at my door."

Travis laughed. "That's our Catie, efficient as always. She even took the time difference into consideration. I'll bet Gage is lookin' at this bombshell right about now, too."

"I was just about to call you. That auction was the other night, wasn't it?"

There was a tiny pause. "So?"

Slade's eyebrows shot skyward. "Trav, my man, don't be so testy."

"I'm not being anything. I called to discuss this invitation."

"What's to discuss? I ain't goin'."

"I'll just bet your high-priced architectural clients love that down-home talk."

"They're never lucky enough to hear it, and stop changing the subject. How'd the auction go?"

"It went. Somebody bought me."

"Lucky lady. She have a name?"

"Alexandra. And that's the end of the story."

"How much did you go for? More than the dude from that other law firm? Was this Alexandra good-lookin'?"

"I went for enough, I beat the pants off the other guy, the lady was okay, if you like the type."

"Oh, my."

"What's that supposed to mean?"

"Well, sounds to me as if my big brother struck out for a change."

"Think again, pal."

"She's there with you, huh?" Slade grinned. "Trav, you old dog, you."

"Slade, do you think you could get your mind on something else?"

"You really want to talk about this birthday party, huh? Well, there's nothing to talk about. I'm not going. I already told you that."

"Jonas is coming up on eighty-five. It's a milestone."

"I don't care if it's a century stone. Why would any of us subject himself to a weekend of misery?"

"It won't be so awful."

"Says you."

"There'll probably be a couple of hundred people there. The old boy won't have the time to chew us up. Besides, I hate to disappoint Caitlin."

"What's with you, Trav? It almost sounds as if you're lookin' to get out of town."

Travis cleared his throat. "It's just—I wouldn't mind a change of scene."

"Woman trouble," Slade said, and sighed.

"Yeah. I guess."

"I might have known."

"No way, kid. You couldn't possibly know. Gage and I are the ones with experience. We've both been married, and don't you forget it."

Slade wondered what his brother would say if he told him that marriage wasn't the only thing that gave a man woman trouble, but he knew better than to set himself up. Besides, he didn't have "woman trouble." A woman had to be part of your life to give you trouble, and Lara wasn't even part of the scenery. He gave what he hoped would pass for a laugh, and told Travis he was trying to change the subject.

"Maybe. Trust me, kid. You don't want to hear the details. Look, about this party—"

"Forget it," Slade said firmly. "I'm sorry, but I'm not going. I really don't have time to go back to Espada right now, okay?"

"That's that, then. Heck, you're too big for me to lock in the feed bin anymore." The brothers chuckled, and then Travis cleared his throat. "Just do me a favor and stay on the line while I phone Gage."

Slade leaned back, put his feet up again and crossed his booted ankles.

"And you just remember, two against one won't do it anymore. Even if Gage says he's going, with bells on, I'm not changing my mind."

"Fair enough."

Slade whistled silently to himself while Travis punched in Gage's number. Gage must have been sitting right next to the telephone, because he picked up right away.

"Baby," he said gruffly, "Natalie, I love you so—"

Travis laughed. Slade did, too.

"I love you, too, precious," Travis said in a falsetto, "but my husband's starting to get suspicious."

"Travis? Is that you?"

Slade grinned. "And me. How are you, bro?"

"I don't believe this! What's with you guys? Are you havin' a reunion out there in California? Or are you both in Boston, livin' it up in that mansion my little brother calls home?"

Travis chuckled. "This three-way brotherly phone call is comin' to you courtesy of the marvels of modern-day science."

"And it's probably the only three-way ever done by telephone," Slade said. The door to his office opened and Betsy entered with his mug of coffee. "Thank you, darlin'," he said, without thinking, saw the look on her face and immediately regretted it.

Travis laughed in his ear. "Don't you darlin' me, pal, or I'll fly straight to that fancy-pants mansion and beat you up the way I used to, when you were twelve and I was thirteen."

"Uh-huh. You an' who else, Mr. Attorney?"

"Me an' Gage. 'Course, it'll have to wait until the sun gets up in the sky apiece, so my brain starts workin' right."

All three brothers laughed. Slade took a sip of his coffee and sat back. He felt better than he had in days.

"Okay, guys," Travis said briskly, "I wish we could avoid the topic but it's time for a reality check."

"The invitation," Slade said. "I agree."

"You got yours, too?" Gage said.

"Was there ever any doubt? It arrived, bright and early." He chuckled. "Bad timing, right, Travis? I mean, yours must have interrupted you and your, ah, your guest."

"Oh, yeah," Travis said lightly, "it did. There's nothing like being awakened with an invitation to purgatory when you're, ah, otherwise involved."

Slade laughed. "The man leads a tough life."

"I'd expect some compassion from you, kid," Travis said

with a smile in his voice. "None from Gage, of course. He gave up his freedom years ago. How's my girl, by the way? You still treating her right, or is she about ready to use that pretty head of hers and ditch you for me?"

"She's fine."

Slade's brows lifted. Gage's answer had seemed strained. Travis must have thought so, too.

"You sure?"

"Yeah," Slade added. "Gage? Is everything okay? You don't sound..."

"Listen, maybe you guys can horse around all day," Gage snapped, "but I've got things to do."

Silence hummed over the lines. Something was wrong, Slade thought, but he knew better than to try to pump Gage for answers. They were all cut from the same cloth. You shared your problems if and when you wanted. Otherwise, not even torture could make you talk.

"Right," he said briskly. "Well, then. Trav already laid out the agenda. We need to decide what we're going to do about this command performance the old man's got planned for the middle of the month."

"Ignore it," Gage said firmly. "I've got—"

"Things to do," Travis said. "I know. And I don't have any greater desire to go back to Espada for a dress rehearsal of King Lear than either of you guys, but—"

"I hate to tell you this, my man," Slade said, "but this is Texas we're talking about, not Stratford-on-Avon."

"What I meant was that Jonas is starting to feel mortal."

Slade snorted. "Our father's figuring on making it to one hundred, and you know what? My money's on him."

"Still, I bet he's looking around, taking stock of that little spread of seven zillion acres he calls home, sweet home, and figuring it's time he made plans on how to divvy up the kingdom."

"Well, I don't need to spend a miserable weekend at Espada to know that I don't give a damn how he does it," Gage said gruffly. "You two enjoy the party without me."

Slade could feel Travis waiting for him to say something. Dammit, he was making him feel guilty about cutting out on Catie, and leaving Trav to face the old man all by himself. He flipped the pages in his appointment book, searching for something substantive. A trip. A conference. Anything...

His stomach dipped. He'd almost forgotten. There it was, in black-and-white. His meeting with Dobbs.

"I can't," he said. "I'm going to be in Baltimore that weekend."

"Or in the Antarctic," Travis said, "anywhere it takes to avoid this shindig, right?"

"Wrong," Slade said—and hesitated. If he went to Espada, he couldn't go to Baltimore. He wouldn't have to spend two days in the same city as Lara, thinking about her, wondering where she was and who she was with... "Listen," he said, with all the conviction he could muster, "I just put in eight weeks on plans for a new bank."

"Dammit, Slade." Travis took a deep breath, then blew it out. "Sorry, kid. I have no right to twist your arm."

"Forget it. Truth is..."

Slade hesitated. The truth was, he really could blow off the Baltimore weekend. A quick meeting, just to touch bases, would be enough. Ted or Jack could go in his place. Dobbs would understand. Who wouldn't? An eighty-fifth birthday celebration was a big thing. And it wasn't cowardice making him do it, either. Catie had planned a big party. Gage sounded definite about not attending. Could he really let Travis get trapped at Espada for a couple of days, without moral support?

Slade sat up straight. "The truth is," he said briskly, "I was lying through my teeth. I can get out of the Baltimore trip."

"Amazing," Gage said. "Three grown men, all of us falling over our own feet in a rush to keep clear of the place where we grew up."

"The thing is," Travis said, "eighty-five is a pretty impressive number."

"The old man was never impressed by other numbers," Gage said bitterly. "Your eighteenth birthday. Slade's two years in grad school."

"Or your fifth anniversary party. I know, but what the hell, gentlemen, we're bigger than that, right? Besides, we're young, he's old. That's a simple fact. And then there's Caitlin."

"Trav got that right," Slade said. "I do hate to disappoint her."

"Me, too," Gage muttered, "but I just don't see a choice here."

"Right," Travis said. "There isn't any choice. We have to show up. We're not kids anymore. Jonas can't get under our skin and make us miserable. And think of the plus side. We get to swap war stories and put a smile on Catie's face at the same time. Is that really so much to ask?"

"I'm in," Slade said.

"Not me," Gage said. "I don't have a weekend to spare."

"Gage," Travis said, "look—"

"No, you look! I'm too busy for this stuff. I have some sensitive things going on here. You got that, or do I have to put it on a billboard in Times... Oh, hell. I'm sorry. I didn't mean to yell. But I can't go. I just can't."

"Sure," Travis said, after a minute.

"Understood," Slade said, a beat later. "Well..."

There was silence, the sound of a throat being cleared. "Well," three voices said, and then there were hurried goodbyes and the brothers all disconnected. Slade waited a second, then punched the button that automatically dialed Gage's number.

"Are you okay?" he said, without any preliminaries.

"I'm fine," Gage said, in a voice that didn't sound fine at all.

"You sure? Because if you need anything—"

"I'll call you."

Slade frowned. "Just remember that." He disconnected, waited a minute, then hit the button to phone Travis. "I called him back," he said, without bothering to say hello.

"Uh-huh. So did I."

"Something's wrong, Trav. I've never heard Gage sound like that."

"Yeah. But whatever it is, he doesn't want to talk about it."

"Trav? You don't think there could be trouble between Gage and Natalie, do you?"

"No way. That marriage was made in heaven. Natalie's wonderful." Travis's tone flattened. "She's not the sort of woman who'd ever make a man jump through hoops. She's like an open book. No games. No secrets."

And no attitude that said, "You were good enough to sleep with but now I can't bear the sight of you," Slade thought, and forced a laugh.

"Tell me about it," he said.

"They're all impossible. They run hot, they run cold. A man never knows what to expect."

"You've got that right," Slade said darkly. "No matter what you say or do, it's never enough." He hesitated. Now that he thought about it, Travis sounded pretty glum, too. "Trav? Uh, are we talking about your ex?"

"No, we're not. And, before you ask, I don't feel like discussing it any further."

Slade sighed. Three grown men with problems, and he'd have bet his life the problems all wore perfume.

"Okay," he said, trying to sound unconcerned, "suit yourself, pal."

"Slade?" Travis's voice softened. "I'm looking forward to seeing you, kid."

Slade smiled. "Yeah," he said, and cleared his throat. "Yeah, Trav. Me, too."

He hung up the phone, swung his chair around and gazed out the window at the river. Sighing, he steepled his fingers against his lips. He hadn't wanted to go back to Texas but now he was almost looking forward to it.

A weekend with the old Los Lobos pack—Gage, and Travis and, once her mother had married Jonas, Caitlin had become a pack member, too.

Slade smiled. Hey, it was just what he needed. Swimming in the creek. Sprawling in the grass for some lazy talk. Goofing around on the deck. And, best of all, having a logical reason not to keep that appointment in Baltimore.

Not that he was afraid of seeing Lara Stevens again. It was just that a man who wanted to hang onto his sanity could do nicely without any further run-ins with a woman who seemed intent on messing not just with his sex drive, but with his head.

CHAPTER FIVE

"MS. STEVENS?"

Lara looked up from the notes she'd been reading. Her secretary stood in the doorway, smiling ruefully.

"Don't tell me," Lara said, and tossed down her pencil.

Nancy grinned. "Okay, I won't. I'll just point out that you told me to let you know when I was leaving. And, if I'm leaving, it must be six o'clock."

"Yes, okay." Lara sighed, propped her elbows on the desk and cupped her face in her hands. "Thanks, Nancy. Is Mr. Dobbs back yet?"

"No. I just checked. His secretary says the plan is still for Mr. Haggerty to meet you here, and for the two of you to go on to The Flying Fish. Mr. Dobbs will join you as soon as he can."

"Great," Lara said glumly.

"Too bad it's not that Mr. Baron flying in for this appointment."

Lara shot the other woman a look. "Why would you say that?"

"Well, the guy is hunky. I mean, if I had to stay late on a Friday night for a business dinner, I'd at least want to enjoy the view."

"This is a business meeting," Lara said, more sharply than she'd intended. "I mean," she added, softening her words with a smile, "who cares what a man looks like when you're looking at him over a plate of shrimp and discussing the cost difference between marble and granite?"

"Ah, the joys of a romantic evening." Nancy rolled her eyes. "I guess it won't matter even if this Mr. Haggerty ends up bearing an uncanny resemblance to a Wookie."

Lara grinned. "Be careful, or I'll report you to Wookies Anonymous. Good night, Nancy. Say hi to Kevin for me. And have a great weekend."

"Same to you, Ms. Stevens. G'night."

The door swung shut, and Lara let the smile slip from her face. It had been a long week. A long two weeks, actually. The last thing she felt like doing was spending a couple of hours making polite small talk with some guy named Jack Haggerty from Baron, Haggerty and Levine, but she was stuck.

Dobbs had been apologetic when he'd called this morning. He'd launched into a lengthy explanation that came down to the fact that he had a dinner appointment with one of the partners from Slade's firm but that he was going to be delayed and would she kindly greet Mr. Haggerty, take him to The Flying Fish and keep him occupied until he, Dobbs, could join them?

No, Lara had longed to say, sorry, but I can't. I just want to go home, to Michael.

Lara sighed, propped her elbows on the desk again and rubbed her temples.

Yes, she'd said, lying through her teeth, it would be a pleasure.

At least it wouldn't be awful, considering that she'd be dealing with a man named Haggerty and not Baron. If Dobbs had said Slade was flying in, that she'd have to spend even two minutes alone with him, she'd have said no and to hell with the consequences. It wasn't that Slade was a problem. She simply didn't like him. All that ego. That—that disgusting machismo.

She made a face.

It was why he'd come after her and made her suffer the indignity of that kiss. That arrogant, I-am-the-Lord-of-the-castle-and-you-are-my-wench kiss, which, she knew, hadn't been a kiss at all. It had been a stamp of dominance. Of humiliation. It had been Slade's way of getting even, of telling her just what he thought of her—and it had almost worked.

Caught off guard, she'd been easy prey. That was why she'd let him get away with mauling her. Oh, if only she'd had time to make a recovery. Slapped him. Cracked him in the jaw. Better still, put her knee right where it counted.

Lara gave a deep sigh and reached for the telephone.

Amazing, the effect Slade Baron had on her. She was a woman who'd once bought a have-a-heart trap rather than send a rodent to Mouse Heaven, and now she'd spent the best part of the past two weeks lying in bed at night, drifting off to sleep while she thought of ingenious ways—painful ways—to dispose of the insufferable Mr. Baron.

It just infuriated her that she'd stood there and seemed to tolerate his kissing her. If only she'd had time to think. She wouldn't have felt so helpless, wouldn't have heard that roaring in her ears. She definitely wouldn't have ended up clutching his jacket as if her knees had been threatening to give way...

Lara groaned.

Dammit, why lie to herself? Her knees *had* threatened to give way. Slade's kiss had turned her inside out. All he had to do was touch her, and she forgot why she hated him. The macho arrogance. The pathetic male fear of commitment. Not that she wanted commitment from him or any other man but still, she'd never forget that smarmy little speech he'd made while she lay in his arms, all about how great it had been and how they'd have to try to get together sometime...

Lara shut her eyes.

Not that she hadn't deserved it. What she'd done—sleeping with a stranger—had been wrong. Never mind her motives. It had been wrong. Cheap. Immoral. Ugly...

"Stop it," she said sharply, and punched in the number for her home telephone. Mrs. Krauss answered on the first ring.

"It's me," Lara said. "How's my guy?" She listened, smiled and felt her spirits lifting. "That's lovely," she said, and turned her back to the door. "Yes, please. Let me speak to him."

She waited, and then her smile grew soft.

"Michael? How are you, sweetheart?"

"Ma-ma-ma," nine-month-old Michael babbled, and Lara's heart melted as she heard the voice of her son.

"That's right, darling. It's Mama. Have you been a good boy today?"

Michael babbled more nonsense sounds, and Lara laughed.

"I miss you, too, my love. I'm sorry I won't be there to have dinner with you but I promise, we'll have the whole weekend alone. *Mmwah*," she said, making a kissing sound into the phone. "I'll give you more of those when I get home. In the meantime, remember how much I love you."

She hung up the phone, sighed with pleasure—and shot to her feet at the slow, mocking sound of applause.

"Isn't that touching?" a voice drawled.

No, she thought, as she swung around, please, no...

Slade stood in the doorway, arms folded. Her traitorous heart gave a little kick she refused to acknowledge, even as she wondered how much he might have heard.

"Such a charming scene, Ms. Stevens. I'm glad I didn't miss it."

Stay calm, she told herself, just stay calm. "What are you doing here?"

"Who's Michael?"

His voice was cold, his eyes flat. Her mind scrambled from thought to thought, like a mouse trying to escape from a maze. What had he overheard? And why, dammit, why should seeing him again make it so hard to draw a steady breath?

She fought for composure, found at least the trappings of it and looked straight into his eyes.

"I asked you a question, Slade. What are you doing here?"

"Why, Sugar. Is that any way to treat a colleague?"

"My door was closed. You didn't even bother to knock."

"I knocked. You didn't answer. And your guard dog isn't at her desk." He moved toward her, his gaze locked to hers. "Now it's your turn. Who's Michael?"

Don't back up, Lara told herself. Don't let him intimidate you.

"He's—he's just someone I know."

Slade laughed. "'I miss you, too, darling,'" he purred. "'You just remember how much I love you.'" His mouth twisted. "Just someone you know, Sugar? Or another guest in your bed?"

"I don't owe you any explanations. That was a private conversation. You had no right—"

"How many men have you been with? A dozen? A hundred?" Slade's brows drew together. Hell, what was he doing? He'd come here on business, not to see this woman. What did he care, if she was getting it on with a guy named Michael? She could sleep with a battalion, for all he gave a damn. She could laugh with every man she knew, get that sweet tone in her voice with the entire male population of Baltimore...

"Dammit," he snarled, and took the last few steps that brought them face-to-face, "does it turn you on, going from one poor sucker to another?"

"Get out." Her voice trembled. "Get the hell out of my office!"

"Do us both a favor and cut the dramatics. There's no audience to enjoy them."

"Get out or so help me, I'll have security throw you out!"

Slade smiled thinly. "Maybe you better call your boss first and see how he feels about that."

"Mr. Dobbs employs me to deal with this company's finances. He'd never expect me to tolerate your horrible accusations about my private life."

"They're not accusations, Sugar. They're fact." A muscle knotted in his jaw. She flinched as he reached out and ran his index finger over her mouth. "I can vouch for your morals, baby—or maybe I should say, I can vouch that you haven't got any. I slept with you, remember? And we didn't even know each other's names."

"You bastard!"

"Hey, I can't help it if you don't like hearing the truth." Slade's teeth flashed in a mirthless smile. "Unless banking isn't what it used to be, I suspect old Ed's eyes would pop once he heard the story. How you pick up strangers, go to hotels with them and have sex."

Lara hissed with fury. Her hand arced through the air, but Slade caught her wrist and yanked her arm behind her.

"I don't give a damn what you do, or who you do it with. It's just that I have this thing about not wanting to take another man's leavings. And now that I've had time to see you in action, I'm starting to wonder if you weren't still some poor bastard's devoted little wife when you slept with me."

"You're despicable! You're the most horrible man I've ever known."

"And I'll bet you've known plenty." His eyes darkened. "Which takes us ba : to square one. Who's Michael?"

Terror raced through her but she didn't so much as blink. "Michael is none of your business."

"I don't agree."

He tugged her arm higher and she made a little sound in her throat. He knew the pressure was hurting her, that the only way she could lessen it was to move closer to him, and he asked himself, coldly, just what in hell he thought he was doing? He'd never hurt a woman in his life, never wanted to, but, by God, he wanted to do something to this one. Hurt her, the way she'd hurt him when he'd opened the door and heard her all but making love over the telephone to some son of a bitch named Michael. Kiss her, make her remember again how it was to be in his arms, with his mouth hard on hers.

She was close to him now, close enough so he could feel

the softness of her breasts, smell the scent that had driven
him half-crazy on that long-ago night. There was a look in
her eyes that said she was either terrified of him or terrified
of what he made her feel and he knew, with heart-stopping
swiftness, that he could take her right now, just shove her
back against the wall, push up her skirt, rip off her panties
and enter her. And that she'd cry out in passion when he
did.

Except—except, that wasn't what he wanted.

He didn't want to take her in anger. He wanted her to
come to him, to give herself to him, to say—to say—

He let go of her wrist, took a quick step away. Lara
watched as he turned his back to her. His shoulders rose
and fell and she knew he was pulling in deep lungfuls of
air, just as she was.

He'd almost kissed her. She'd seen it in his eyes, in the
sudden angularity of his features. And if he had—if he
had…

He swung toward her, his expression grim.

"My apologies, Ms. Stevens." His tone was as flat as his
eyes. "I have no right to sit in judgment on you. You can't
help what you are any more than the sun can help coming
up in the morning."

Lara stared at him. "You know, you're amazing! You—
you pick me up at an airport, seduce me, tell me it's been
nice and hey, maybe we'll see each other around sometime
and now you think *you* can lecture *me?*" She gave a shaky
laugh. "Sorry, but I don't see any difference between your
actions and mine."

"The hell there isn't." He moved fast, closing the distance between them, grabbing her by the shoulders and half
lifting her from her feet. "You're a junkie, lady. You need
to drive a man crazy, make him say things he curses himself
for in the middle of the night." His hands dropped away
from her and she stumbled back. "And if you want to sleep
with any guy who catches your fancy while you're involved
with some poor sap named Michael, hell, that's your affair."

His mouth twisted. "But I won't play that game, Sugar. I don't rustle another man's stock."

"The Baron version of the Golden Rule." Lara laughed, though tears stung her eyes. "Honestly, I'm impressed. Such morality."

"Just don't come on to me again or you'll regret it. You got that?"

"Me? Come on to you?" Her laughter was real this time, if bitter. "Which one of us just walked through that door and shoved the other against the wall?"

"I did not shove you against—"

"Give me a break, Slade." Lara slapped her hands on her hips. "I'm not stupid. I know what you were thinking. What you wanted to do."

"Yeah." A knowing smile angled across his mouth. "And I could have, Sugar. You would have let me. Hell, you wanted me to do it."

Lara flushed. "You flatter yourself," she said stiffly.

"I believe in honesty. I take it you're familiar with the concept?"

"I'm not going to get drawn into this. Let's go back to the beginning. Why are you here?"

"I have a meeting with your boss."

"What happened to Mr. Haggerty?"

"He couldn't make it. And before that female brain of yours leaps to any conclusions, no, I had no idea I'd end up stuck with you. My appointment was with Dobbs. The first I knew you were involved was when I spoke to him a couple of hours ago, from the plane, and he told me he was going to be delayed."

Lara nodded. There was no way out, not now. Dobbs wasn't here, which made Slade her responsibility—a responsibility she could certainly handle, now that their animosity for each other was in the open.

"That's right," she said briskly. "He's going to join us at the restaurant." She glanced at her watch. "I've arranged for a taxi. It should be downstairs any minute."

"Fine." Slade gave her a long, cool look. It took all her determination not to shuffle her feet.

"What?"

"I was just thinking how remarkable it was. That you look so businesslike, I mean. So—what's that old-fashioned word, Sugar? Demure. That's it. You look demure." A smile curled over his mouth. "That's sure as hell not the way you look when I touch you. You go all to pieces, in my arms."

"You're flattering yourself, if you think you turn me on." She knew she was blushing but she wouldn't give him the pleasure of backing down. "As you so cleverly pointed out, I'm just playing a game. Why don't you think about that, hmm?"

Her smile, she hoped, was the smug equal of his. Without another word, she strode past him to the door.

The captain at The Flying Fish smiled brightly when Lara asked to be shown to the Dobbs table.

"Of course, madam. Sir. This way, please."

The table was outside, on a wide deck overlooking the harbor. The sky was still light but candles already flickered in a silver holder centered on the pale pink tablecloth. It was a romantic setting, not businesslike at all, and Lara paused on the threshold between the main dining room and the deck.

"Is there a problem, madam?"

"I just thought... Do you have a table inside? Where the lighting's better?"

"I'm sorry, madam, but we don't. If you'd care to wait in the bar for half an hour or so, we might have something free...?"

"No." Lara shook her head and told herself to stop being a fool. "No, this will be fine."

Once they were seated, their waiter offered menus but she declined.

"We'll wait for the third member of our party to join us," she said.

"Would you care to order drinks while you wait?"

She began to say no to that, too, and then she thought of what Edwin Dobbs would think about her efforts as hospitality, if she did.

"White wine for me," she said briskly. "Slade?"

"A beer." Slade flashed the waiter a smile. "Something dark, if you have it. I'll go with your recommendation."

They sat in silence for a moment or two. Then Lara cleared her throat.

"How was your flight?"

"Fine." His eyes met hers. "No weather delays, no blizzards—"

"Very amusing. It was just a polite question."

"Ah, I see. We're going to play this scene with sophistication."

"Only because we have to." Lara's eyes flashed. "Believe me, I'd much rather—I'd rather…"

"Shove me over the railing?" He grinned. "Feed me to the fishes?"

"They'd probably spit you out." She folded her hands in her lap. "What happened to Mr. Haggerty?"

"Don't you mean, what did I do to take his place? Shoot him? Chain him to the dungeon floor? Bribe him so I could have the sheer joy of seeing you again?" He reached for a bread stick and took a bite. "I hate to disappoint you, Sugar, but the simple fact is that Jack injured his shoulder playing racquetball this morning."

"How unfortunate."

"I'll tell him you said so. Your warmth and concern will touch him as much as deeply as they touch me."

"Your other partner could have come instead," Lara said, ignoring his sarcasm.

"My oh my, you do think a lot of yourself." Slade leaned forward. "What's going through that head of yours? You think I sabotaged Jack and Teddy, too?" He sat back. "I told you, I came because there wasn't any choice. Jack did in his shoulder and Ted's in New York on business. That's the reason—the only reason—I'm here.''

It was the truth, all right. No way, no how, no time would he have willingly subjected himself to another moment in this babe's company. What man would, unless he got a kick out of being turned on and off like a lightbulb?

''As far as I'm concerned,'' Lara said, glancing at her watch, ''the sooner you're gone, the better.''

''Darlin', you're breakin' my heart. Are you saying you find my company boring?''

''I know this is going to be hard to get your self-centered brain to process, Slade, but there are things I'd rather do than sit here watching you munch your way through the bread sticks.''

''Like cuddling up to—what was his name?''

''What was whose name?''

''The latest man in your life. Michael. That was it, wasn't it?''

''I told you, I don't intend to discuss Michael. I don't intend to talk about my private life at all.''

''You're the one who brought him into the conversation, not me.''

''Me? I never—''

''You were talking about all those things you'd rather be doing than sitting here, trying to be civil.'' A muscle flickered in his jaw but he smiled and reached for his glass. ''Had your evening with Mike all planned, did you? A cozy dinner for two, maybe? Am I right?''

''Yes,'' Lara said, fighting the desire to break into hysterical laughter. She pictured Michael in his high chair, waving a spoon of mashed potatoes in the air, grinning at her through a carrot-puree mustache. ''Oh, definitely. A cozy dinner was what we'd intended.''

''Do you live with him?''

''Yes,'' she said, getting into the spirit of things, ''yes, I do.''

Slade's mouth thinned. "What was he doing? Waiting in the wings while you divorced your husband?"

Lara took a bread stick from the basket and bit into it. "That's none of your business."

"Does he know about me?" he said coldly, his eyes locked on hers.

No, she thought, oh, no. And he never would.

"Why should he?" she said with a puzzled smile. "You're nothing to him."

"Old Mike might disagree with that, if he knew what happens whenever we're alone."

"Nothing happens."

"Is that what you call it, when you turn soft in my arms?"

"Dammit, Slade—"

"Do you do that for him, too? Melt, I mean. And make those little sounds when he puts his hands—"

Lara tossed down the bread stick and shot to her feet. "This is impossible!"

"Ms. Stevens? Is there a problem?"

Oh Lord!

Lara swung around and stared dumbly at Edwin Dobbs. He was smiling politely, but his eyes were cool and questioning.

"No," Lara said quickly. "I—no, there's—there's—"

"Edwin." Slade kicked back his chair and rose to his feet. "It's good to see you again."

Dobbs hesitated, then took Slade's extended hand. "Slade." His gaze went from Lara to Slade. "I'm, ah, I'm sorry to be late."

"That's okay," Slade said easily, as they all settled into their chairs. "Although Ms. Stevens—Lara—was growing concerned with, ah, with the service. Our, uh, our waiter took our drinks order and disappeared."

"They must be having an off night." Dobbs relaxed into his seat. "Well, let's hope the chef's on target, anyway. This place does extraordinary crab cakes. And the blackened redfish?'' He smiled and kissed his fingertips. "It's like poetry. Just the barest kiss of spices."

"The barest kiss. Sounds charming," Slade said pleasantly. "Isn't that right, Lara?"

Lara looked across the table at him. "Yes," she said, after the briefest hesitation. "Yes, it does."

And she buried her face in the menu.

Would the evening never end?

Dobbs and Slade chatted easily, about the new building, about the city, about everything, until Lara wondered if they'd ever stop talking. She smiled until her jaw hurt, moved her food around her plate, sipped her wine and managed to say yes, no, and maybe whenever the time seemed right.

Finally, just when she knew she'd scream if she had to tolerate another minute, Dobbs looked at his watch, sighed with what seemed genuine reluctance and signaled for the check.

"Slade?" he said, as they stood outside the restaurant. "Are you staying in town or are you flying back to Boston tonight?"

"I'm flying to Texas, Edwin. That birthday party, remember?"

"Oh. Yes, of course. Well, then, since I'm going the other way, perhaps you and Ms. Stevens might want to share a cab. I believe you head in that direction, don't you, my dear?"

"No," Lara said quickly. "I mean—I mean, I don't see—"

"I don't see it as a problem, either," Slade said politely. His hand closed on her elbow, his fingers tightening when she tried to jerk away. "Thank you for dinner, Edwin. I'll have my office fax you the name of that interior designer I mentioned."

"Wonderful," Dobbs said, and beamed. "Ms. Stevens, good night. I know I'm leaving you in good hands."

"In good hands, indeed," Lara snapped, as soon as the door to the taxi slammed behind her. She pulled her arm from Slade's grasp, scooted across the seat and as far into the corner as she could manage. "I almost told him the truth, that I'd rather walk than share a cab with you."

"What's the problem, Sugar?" Slade leaned back, folded his arms and stretched out his long legs. "Don't you trust yourself not to jump my bones in such a confined space?"

"Jump your bones?" Lara shot him a furious look. "The only time I'd want to jump your bones is if I were wearing hobnailed boots."

She folded her arms, too, and stared out the side window in silence until they reached her house.

Slade reached past her and opened the door. "Shall I see you in?" he said, all but oozing politeness.

Lara didn't bother answering. She stepped onto the pavement, slammed the door as hard as she could and hurried up the walk. Not even knowing she was about to enter her own private little world eased her rage.

Mrs. Krauss opened the door before she could turn her key in the lock.

"It's a good thing you're back," she said crossly. "A woman with a baby shouldn't keep such late hours."

"It was business, Mrs. Krauss." Lara tried to sound polite. It wasn't easy to find someone reliable to care for Michael. Mrs. Krauss was her third attempt in as many months. "I'm sorry I kept you. As always, I'll pay you double for the extra time. Thank you for staying, and I'll see you Monday morning."

"Monday night I'm leaving for Florida." Mrs. Krauss jammed a baseball cap on her graying hair. "My sister's sick. Don't know when I'll be back."

"No." Lara hurried after the older woman. "You can't do that, Mrs. Krauss! You can't just—just leave me in the lurch!"

"I'll call, when I get back," Mrs. Krauss said, and slammed the door.

Lara stared after her retreating figure. Then she slumped back against the wall and groaned. Now what? The day care centers had endless waiting lists. Not that she wanted to leave Michael in a place where he'd be one solitary little boy among many. It was bad enough he didn't have a full-time mother or a grandmother or aunt who even pretended to care about him...

Lara blew out her breath, locked the door, then climbed the stairs to the second floor.

That was tomorrow's problem. She'd phone the agencies and, if worse came to worse, she'd call in sick on Monday. She had meetings but she could reschedule them. Nothing was as important as Michael.

He was in his blue-and-white bedroom, fast asleep, tucked into his crib with his beloved teddy bear curled in his arm. One glance at her sleeping son, and the tensions of the impossible evening seeped from Lara's bones.

Her bedroom adjoined his. Quietly she kicked off her black pumps, shed her suit and blouse, traded the identifying armor of her career for an old cotton robe and bare feet. This was the only career she wanted now, the only one that mattered, she thought as she lifted Michael gently from his crib.

It wasn't possible to be with him full-time. She needed her job to support her little family but oh, how she envied the handful of women she saw in the park on those rare, wonderful weekdays she stayed home to care for her baby.

Michael stirred in her arms.

"Hello, sweetheart," she whispered.

He blinked, then opened his eyes. He gave a bleary smile and she caught her breath as she looked at her son.

He had his father's black hair. His nose, and even his chin. There was no mistaking those smoky-gray eyes...

There was no pretending her child was not Slade Baron's son.

Fear rolled in her blood. What would Slade do if he found

out? The games he thought she'd played were nothing compared with this one. This game had the highest stakes of all.

Michael yawned and murmured sleepily as she settled in the rocking chair. Minutes slipped by, and memories, as she snuggled him to her breast. It had been hard, at first. Putting in for the transfer from Atlanta. Inventing a husband and a divorce because that made for fewer questions. Being alone, always alone...

The doorbell rang.

Lara's head jerked up at the sound.

The doorbell, at this hour?

The bell rang again, and Michael—asleep now—stirred in her arms.

She rose from the rocker, carefully lay him in his crib. It had to be Mrs. Krauss. Maybe it was just as well she was leaving. She was good with Michael—she seemed to be, anyway. But she was gruff. And forgetful. Last week, she'd been halfway home before she'd realized she'd left her handbag in the kitchen.

The bell shrilled a third time as she ran down the stairs. "Mrs. Krauss," she said impatiently as she cracked the door, "for goodness sakes, you're going to wake—"

It wasn't Mrs. Krauss. It was Slade.

Lara slammed the door in his face. At least, she tried to, but he was quicker and stronger, and he'd had enough of playing games to last him a lifetime. She pushed, he pushed back, and just that easily, he was inside the house.

Slade knew he'd said he never chased a woman who belonged to another man, and he didn't. But Lara had spent the evening making him feel as if he were a disease she'd contracted instead of a man she'd made passionate love with through a long winter's night, and the reason for it was somebody named Michael. Well, he'd decided he wasn't leaving Baltimore until he had a look at this paragon of manly virtue—and maybe, just for kicks, flattened the bastard's nose.

A couple of beers at the bar where the cabbie had dropped

him, followed by a walk around the block four or five times, had convinced him that was a sensible, even a necessary, thing to do.

Nobody, especially not Lara, was going to stop him.

"Where is he?" Slade growled, and kicked the door shut.

"Who?" Lara said. Michael, she thought, oh, Michael, don't make a sound.

"Do us both a favor, okay?" Slade brushed past her and peered into the living room. "I know he's here, you know he's here. Let him come out and face me like a man."

"You're drunk," she said, and danced in front of him.

His smile glittered with hostility. "I tried, but trust me, Sugar, I'm stone-cold sober."

"I'll call the police. And don't bother threatening me, Slade. I don't give a damn if this ends up in court. Nobody at Beaufort will blame me for calling the cops after you broke into my house."

"Broke in? Me?" He gave a harsh laugh, stepped around her and looked in the kitchen. "We had dinner, took a cab and you invited me in. If you deny it, I'll just have to tell old Ed all about you and me and that Denver hotel." The living room was empty, and the tiny dining room. Slade started up the stairs. "Dammit, where is he? And don't lie to me, Lara. I know your precious Michael is here. You almost flew out of that cab, you were so damned eager to be with him."

"All right." Lara moistened her lips. "He's here. He's— he's sleeping. And if—if you wake him, he's going to be angry. He'll be hard to deal with."

Slade laughed as he strode down the hallway. It wasn't a pretty sound. "That's fine, Sugar. The mood I'm in, I'd just as soon lover-boy was hard to deal with tonight."

"Slade, please." God, oh God, he was at Michael's bedroom. Breathless, she cut in front of him again and barred the door with her body. "Don't. Don't!"

She whimpered as he clasped her waist and lifted her out

of his way. She could feel the anger humming through his blood.

"Time to wake up, Michael my man," Slade said, and switched on the light.

With that, she could fool the anger brimming through her blood.

"I can be like this, Michael my love," Connie said, and put out the light.

CHAPTER SIX

SLADE'S flight to Dallas had already left, but there was another plane boarding just as he got to the airport.

He bought his ticket, ran for the gate and made it with seconds to spare. It occurred to him that he might end up standing around the Dallas airport, waiting to catch a connecting flight to Austin. Hell, he thought wryly, why not? Airports had been big in his life lately.

All he wanted right now was to put as much distance as possible between himself and what he'd just stumbled into.

A baby. Lara had a baby. He could hardly absorb it but he knew the image would be burned into his brain forever. The room, illuminated like a stage when the curtain lifts as he turned on the light. The crib, bathed in the glow.

And the kid, asleep in the crib.

Lord, the kid.

For a minute that hovered on the brink of eternity, nothing moved. He stood there. Lara stood there. Then, finally, she made a sound that was almost a moan. When she did, he swung toward her.

"You have a child," he'd said.

Slade groaned and put his head back. What a brilliant statement that had been.

Right about then the kid woke, sat up and clutched the crib railing. It was a boy, he'd thought numbly; he could tell by the fuzzy blue thing that covered it right down to its feet.

The kid had stared at him with a pair of huge, smoky gray eyes for a long minute, not crying, not making a sound, just—just sort of checking him out, if such a thing were possible. Slade had stared right back, a chill running down

82

his spine. Lara had a son. It was all he seemed capable of thinking. Then the kid's face dissolved and it began to cry. Lara flew past him, snatched the child in her arms.

"Michael," she crooned, "sweetheart, it's okay. Mama's here, Michael. Don't be afraid."

Slade, with a tongue that felt too big for his mouth, took a step back.

"Lara?" he said, and she turned to him, her face white, her eyes wild.

"Get out," she'd whispered, and then her voice rose, balanced on the edge of hysteria, and she'd screamed the words again...

Not that she had to.

He'd done just what she said, got out as fast as his feet could carry him, got out without looking back.

Slade closed his eyes. This changed everything. It had been bad enough, knowing Lara had belonged to other men. A hundred of them, for all he knew. But she had a child. Another man had given her a child...

"Hi."

He jerked his head around and saw a woman slipping into the seat beside his.

"Is this taken? I haven't noticed anybody sitting in it, so I thought—"

"No, I don't think it is."

She smiled. "Well, then, I'm Janet."

"Janet," Slade said. "Pretty name. Pretty voice. Pretty face, too." He cleared his throat. "The thing is, Janet, you'd be wasting your time. Or I'd be wasting it for you."

Her smile froze. "I beg your pardon?"

"It's a long, involved story, Janet, and I'm not much in the mood to tell it. So have a nice flight, and just don't expect anything from me. How's that sound?"

The woman sprang to her feet. "You're crazy!"

Slade gave a short, harsh laugh. "Yeah," he said wearily, "that, too."

He turned his face to the window. The image of the

baby's face flashed against the dark glass. A shock of inky-black hair. Eyes the color of smoke...

Slade grabbed for the headset, jammed it on and punched in a track of hard, heavy rock. Anything, to stop his brain from whirling. Anything, he thought, and put his head back and closed his eyes.

He got to Espada in the middle of the night.

Carmen heard him come in the back door.

"It's Slade," he said, before she could shriek and set off enough noise to blast the entire house awake.

She smiled, waddled toward him and enclosed him in her arms for a hug.

"You are no different than when you were a boy," she said, holding him at arm's length. "Always sneaking into the house long after others were in bed."

"And you always covered for me with my old man." He smiled, kissed her cheek. "Just look at you. You're more beautiful than ever."

"And you are as good a liar as ever," she said, but she blushed. "Are you hungry? I can heat something from dinner, or make you a sandwich, if you prefer."

"All I want is a hot shower and a night's sleep. Is anybody else here yet?"

"Your brothers, you mean? Travis flies in tomorrow, as does Gage."

Slade grinned. "Gage, too, huh?" He bent down, kissed the housekeeper's cheek again. "You know what, Carmen? It's good to be home."

And it was.

It was even better the next morning, when he turned from the sideboard in the dining room just in time to see Catie flying toward him.

"Slade," she cried, and flung herself into his outstretched arms. "Carmen said you were here. When did you get in? Why didn't you wake me? Isn't it wonderful, that Travis and Gage are coming in today?"

"Whoa. That's too many questions before I've had my coffee. It's good to see you, darlin'."

"I'm so happy you're all going to be here." Caitlin kissed him again, then stepped away and poured coffee for them both. "Right up until the last second," she said, handing a cup to him, "I wasn't really sure any of you guys would show."

"And risk having you come after us with that mean little quirt of yours?" Slade grinned. "You don't know your own power, honey."

"Sure I do." Catie grinned over the rim of her cup. "I'm lean. I'm mean..."

"You're part of the team. The old Los Lobos cheer. Damned if I hadn't almost forgotten it."

"Well, not me. When I think of the rough time you all gave me before you let me join the pack..."

"You were a girl."

"How astute." Caitlin wrinkled her nose. "But I could ride a horse and swim that rough stretch in the creek as well as you guys by the time my mother and I had been here six months."

"Yeah. But you were still a girl."

"It's just a good thing the three of you idiots finally figured out that girls were okay."

Slade's smile tilted. "You are, anyway."

Caitlin's slender eyebrows arched. "Uh-oh."

"Uh-oh?"

"As in, uh-oh, that sounds ominous. Don't tell me my handsome brother's having woman trouble."

"Me?" Slade put down the cup, went to the sideboard and spooned some scrambled eggs onto his plate. "You know me, honey. I love 'em and leave 'em."

"You didn't answer my question."

Slade sighed. His stepsister could be persistent. "I wouldn't call it 'trouble.' Just a, uh, a rough patch."

"What happened? Were you the one who got loved and left this time?"

He gave a choked laugh. "Catie, sweetheart, it's not that I don't appreciate your interest, but—"

"But you don't want to talk about it."

"There's nothing to talk about. I told you, I just hit a little bump in the road."

"Well, as you so cleverly pointed out, I'm female. Maybe I can give you some perspective on your, uh, your bump in the road."

Slade looked at his sister. Catie's smile radiated innocence. Oh, yeah. He could just imagine telling her about Lara. Well, he'd say, You see, kid, there's this babe I went to bed with and then didn't see for a long time, until just a couple of weeks ago. The thing is, I can't seem to keep my hands off her and it's the same with her, even though we don't much like each other—and oh, did I mention, I just found out she's got a kid? A little boy, with a thatch of inky-black hair...

"Slade?" Caitlin put her hand on his arm. "Slade, what's the matter? You look as if you just saw a ghost."

"Nothing. Nothing's the matter. I'm fine." He took a deep breath and flashed a smile. "My life's been crazy lately, that's all. A couple of days with you and Travis and Gage, I'll be fine."

"Amazin'," a deep voice drawled, "how my own flesh and blood jes' managed to leave any mention of his daddy out of that heartwarmin' little speech."

Slade stiffened and turned around. Jonas Baron stood in the doorway, as leathery, straight and tall as ever.

"Father," Slade said politely, "it's good to see you."

Jonas grinned. "Bull patties."

Bull patties, indeed, Slade thought.

Some things, at least, never changed.

By the time Travis arrived, Slade was feeling almost his old self again.

He wasn't so sure about Trav, who almost snapped his

head off when he made a joke about Travis being knee-deep in blondes.

"What's that supposed to mean?" Travis demanded, in a way that had once meant they were going to end up rolling around on the ground while they pummeled each other.

That, at least, had changed. Instead of decking him, Travis sighed, mumbled an apology and they laughed it off. Travis did, anyway. Slade just pretended to. Something was eating at his older brother, something female, probably, but Travis didn't want to talk about it. Well, that was understandable. What was the sense in discussing the problems you had with women when there was no logical way to solve them? Women were like crossword puzzles with some of the clues missing. Just when you thought you had a handle on figuring them out, you realized you didn't.

Gage arrived next and that was another shock, finding out that Natalie had left him. What was happening to the old Los Lobos pack, anyway? Still, they ended up laughing and joking, surviving a session with the old man that made it clear Travis was right when he'd figured Jonas was thinking about who would inherit Espada. The thing was, none of them wanted it. Catie did, and she deserved it, but the old s.o.b. couldn't get past the fact that she wasn't a Baron by birth.

"Lucky Catie," Slade muttered as he, Gage and Travis all trooped out to the old barn, and up to the hayloft.

After a while, their mood lightened. It was like old times, sitting around and joking about this and that. A guy named Grant Landon joined them. He was the old man's lawyer but Gage knew him, from a long time back. Landon turned out to be okay—and damned if he didn't have problems with his wife, just like Gage.

What was it, Slade wondered, as he dressed for Jonas's birthday party, that made women so damned difficult to understand?

Natalie, walking out on Gage? Slade shook his head as he did the studs on his dress shirt. And from what the

Landon guy said, the odds on his marriage hitting the rocks had been every bit as unbelievable.

Slade picked up his tie, drew it around his neck and turned toward the mirror.

Travis, at least, wasn't in trouble half as deep. He had something on his mind, all right, and it probably was a woman, but it had to be temporary. No way Trav would get himself seriously involved again, considering what he'd gone through the first time.

Hell, Slade thought, leaning closer to the mirror and frowning as he tried to get the bow tie right, nobody who'd grown up in the Baron household would get into a serious relationship, not unless he was nuts. Except for Gage, that was, and even so, look at the mess he was in now.

"Dammit," Slade said.

The tie just wouldn't lie right. One end was too long, the other too short. He could go down the hall, to Catie's room, ask her to fix it. She knew how to do bows. Women usually did. What about Lara? Could she tie a bow? Had she ever tied one for her ex-husband? He'd never asked her the guy's name, or what he did...

Or what was the color of his hair, or his eyes.

"Dammitall," Slade snarled. He yanked the tie off, jammed it into his pocket, threw open the door and went downstairs, to join the party.

Two hours later, he was having a wonderful time. That was what he told himself, anyway. If he said it often enough, he figured it just might turn out to be true.

It was what he told Catie, when she danced by in the arms of that old snake, cousin Leighton, and what he told Leighton's son, Gray, who was about as unlike his old man as it was possible to be. It was what he said to Marta, too, when he kissed her cheek and told her she was the most beautiful woman in the room.

"That's a charming lie," his stepmother said, smiling back at him, "but, coming from the best-looking man here,

I'll treasure it." She looped her arm through his. "Why aren't you dancing? Every female over the age of puberty has her eye on you, just waiting for you to be so kind as to break her heart."

Slade laughed. "I promise, I'll do my best to oblige. What about you? How come my father let you out of his sight?"

Marta smiled as she took a flute of champagne from a passing waiter.

"You know Jonas. He's gone off somewhere for a bit of chitchat with some of his cronies." She sipped some of the wine, then looked up at him again. "Is everything all right?"

"Why do women always ask that question?" Slade dredged up what he hoped was an easy smile. "First Catie asks me if I'm okay, now you." He put his hand over Marta's. "Yes. I'm fine. I've just been busy lately, flying back and forth from one job to another."

"I didn't mean to pry, Slade. It's just that you looked... Well, never mind." Marta laughed gently. "You're right. We women can be impossible. We look for trouble even when there isn't any, your father says."

"Well, for once I agree with him." Slade looked past his stepmother, to a little knot of men crowded together. "What's going on over there? Looks like a football huddle."

Marta swung around, followed his gaze and laughed.

"It's my daughters. They're in the center of that—what did you call it? A huddle?"

"Your daughters? I haven't seen them in years. Three cute little girls, as I recall. Sam, and Mandy, and Carrie."

Marta's eyes twinkled. "These days, you can only call them that on pain of death. It's Samantha. Amanda. And Carin, if you please. Come on. Let me take you over."

She drew him toward the little crowd and it parted reluctantly, revealing three young women beautiful enough to make a man's heart stop.

"Girls, this is Jonas's youngest son, Slade. I don't know if you recall meeting him before, so let me introduce you. Slade, this is Samantha."

Samantha was a redhead. "Hi," she said, and flashed a dimpled smile.

"And Amanda."

Amanda was blond. "Hello," she said, and offered a smile that was intriguingly cool.

"And this is Carin, my eldest daughter."

Carin was brunette and businesslike. "Nice to meet you," she said, and stuck out her hand.

"Well, well, well," Slade said, and smiled, and for the first time he thought maybe, just maybe, he really might start to enjoy the evening.

He tried. Marta's daughters tried, too. But as lovely as the trio of sisters were, there was no chemistry. One by one, they drifted away, with Carin the last to leave.

"Whoever she is," she said gently, "you have to forget about her."

Slade thought of looking baffled, of offering a denial. In the end, he nodded, jammed his hands deep into his trouser pockets and said that was great advice, if only he could figure out a way to take it.

He danced with one gorgeous woman after another. He had another conversation with Gray and made plans to get together for dinner the next time they were both in New York. He ate canapés and drank champagne and, at last, weary of keeping a smile plastered to his face, he went outside, down to the lowest level of the three decks that fell like a waterfall from the rear of the house to the gardens, found a shadowed corner and a quiet bench and sat down.

Maybe out here, with the quiet of the night around him, he could sort out what was happening to his life...but the smell of expensive cigar smoke intruded.

Slade frowned and rose to his feet. "Father?"

Jonas's deep chuckle sounded from the darkness to his left. "The Havana gave me away, huh?"

Slade turned and looked at his father. Jonas was leaning his elbows on the deck railing, the cigar clamped between his teeth.

"I thought you were in the house. Marta said you were closeted with some of your cronies."

"I was." The older man took the cigar from his mouth, sniffed it appreciatively, then bit down lightly on it again. "What're you doin' out here, boy? Don't you like all that fancy stuff goin' on inside?"

Slade smiled and leaned his elbows on the railing alongside Jonas.

"It's one fine party," he said.

"It is that. But you know Catie. She takes it into her head to do somethin', she does it right."

"She loves you." Slade looked at his father and arched one dark eyebrow. "Despite your best attempts to convince her otherwise."

Jonas nodded. "Almost as if she were my own flesh and blood."

"Flesh and blood doesn't count for everything, Father."

"It does, when you get to the point where you can stand on the road and see clear to the end of it."

Slade laughed. "You'll outlive all of us."

"I won't outlive Espada, that's for certain, which is why it's got to go to somebody who's a Baron."

"Catie's better than a Baron. She loves you, and she loves this place."

"You think I'm stupid?" Jonas waved his hand to ward off any protest. "I know all that."

"Well, then…"

"Well, then, what? Speak up, boy. I ain't no mind reader."

Slade's jaw tightened. "No," he said coldly, "you aren't. If you were, you'd know that if you call me 'boy' one more time, I'm just liable to—"

"Well, will you look at that?" Jonas chuckled, tossed away his cigar and turned towards his son. "You got some gumption left in you, I see. That pansy stuff you do ain't completely destroyed your backbone.''

"I design office buildings," Slade said through his teeth, despising himself for sounding defensive. "Damned fine ones, which you'd know if you occasionally took your nose out of your—"

"The one in *Noo* York City ain't bad a-tall."

Slade blinked. "The Stahl building. You've seen it?"

"'Course, I like the one in Philadelphia better. Nice lines to that, what do you call it, that indoor park thing with the fancy waterfalls on all them levels?"

"An atrium." Slade heard the disbelief in his own voice and he cleared his throat. "When did you see my buildings?"

"Oh, I get around." Jonas grinned at him. "Man wants to see what his offspring are up to, even if he don't approve."

"Well." Slade told himself to say something intelligent but nothing would come. "Well," he said again, "that's— that's very interesting."

"You'd be surprised what a man thinks, when he gets to be my age."

"You're not old," Slade said, and meant it. "Hell, Pop, I hope I look half as good as you when Catie tosses me my eighty-fifth birthday party."

He waited for his father to chuckle but the old man didn't. Instead he reached into his hip pocket and took out a silver flask.

"Bourbon," he said, unscrewing the top. "Have a sip."

Bourbon, Slade thought, of course. Jonas loved the stuff, which was probably why his sons all hated it. Still, he took the flask, nodded his thanks and tilted it to his lips, though he let only the slightest amount of liquid trickle down his throat. He couldn't recall ever sharing a companionable moment with his father before and he wasn't going to ruin it over a taste of bourbon.

"Thanks," he said, and tried not to shudder.

Jonas's teeth flashed in a quick grin. "You're welcome." He took a long swallow, sighed with satisfaction and put the top back on the flask. "So, you figure your stepsister's gonna throw you a big party the day you turn eighty-five."

Slade laughed. "Something like that."

"Why should she?"

Jonas's voice was cool. Slade frowned and looked at him. "I'm just joking."

"I know you are, but think about it. Why should she do that? By then, she'll have a husband of her own. Children. Probably even grandchildren." He reached into his breast pocket, took out another cigar, bit off the tip and spat it into the darkness. "You want somebody to give a damn what happens to you as the years go by, boy, you need to have yourself some sons." Jonas took a gold lighter from his pocket, flicked it on and slowly lit his cigar. "Unless," he said lazily, "you don't need that advice."

"I don't. I'm capable of planning my own life, Father. I have been, ever since I turned eighteen."

The old man blew out a plume of cigar smoke. "What I meant was, maybe you don't need that advice because you already started arrangin' for some heirs."

Slade's heart seemed to kick against his ribs. "What are you talking about?"

"Babies." Jonas puffed out a series of perfect smoke rings. "You know what those are, boy, and you know how to make 'em. Leastways, you been practicin' ever since Dan Archer's wife gave you that extra-special birthday present all them years ago."

"Never mind that," Slade said tightly. Without thinking, he reached out and grasped the older man's arm. "What kind of crack was that, Father? About me already producing heirs?"

"I didn't say that, exactly."

"What did you say, exactly?"

"I simply said that a man who beds a lot of women is liable to find he may have left one of 'em with more than happy memories." Jonas looked pointedly at his son's hand, wrapped around his arm. "You gonna rip that sleeve off'n my tux, son? Won't mean a damn to me. I hate wearin' the thing, but Marta might mind me comin' back into my own party lookin' like I been stomped by a mean bull."

Slade followed his father's gaze. It looked like he had a death grip on his biceps. Slowly, deliberately, he let go.

"Not that it's any of your business," he said stiffly, "but I'm always careful about protection. For the woman's sake, and for my own."

Jonas shrugged. "All it takes is one time. Just once." His voice roughened, and the easy Texas drawl disappeared. "If men and women play around in bed, they end up payin' the price."

"Don't you think I know that? I just said, I'm always careful."

Always, except the time he'd taken Lara to that hotel. His hunger had been so deep, his need so intense...it had driven all rational thought from his head. No, she'd said, when he'd wanted to buy condoms, no, it's not necessary...

Now she had a child. A son, with black hair and gray eyes, and a face so familiar, even in its childish innocence, that it might have been his own. He didn't know the boy's age but it looked right. He was no expert on kids but Jack had a nephew who was nine, ten months old.

Yeah. The size was just about the same.

Slade felt as if a fist had landed in his gut. He wrapped his hands around the railing, bent forward and took a gasping breath. There was no use telling himself not to think about it. He knew what he'd seen, what it meant—and what he had to do.

He turned to Jonas. "Pop..."

But there was nobody standing next to him. His father was gone. The only lingering sign he'd been there was the glowing stub of a Cuban cigar.

CHAPTER SEVEN

SLADE stood on the deck, alone, and stared blindly into the shadowy darkness.

An owl cried out in the distance, its eerie call piercing the silence. He thought of the terror the sound must strike into the hearts of the tiny night-creatures, of how they'd freeze, then scuttle desperately for sanctuary. Their flight would be useless. Nothing would elude the owl's fierce eye and the bite of its razor-sharp talons.

Slade wrapped his hands tightly around the railing, until his knuckles shone white.

He had fathered a child. A son. And Lara had not told him. She'd been determined to keep his parenthood a secret but he knew it, now, and she would no more escape his fury than the denizens of the night would escape the owl.

Did she think he wouldn't give a damn that he'd helped create a life?

His plans hadn't included having children. Children needed stability. They needed—they deserved—the love of two parents. He'd grown up believing it, knowing, in his heart, that he'd missed something wonderful and knowing, too, that marriage—all the forever after nonsense, the hearts and flowers—were not for him.

Everyone thought he was just a carefree bachelor, cruising from woman to woman for the pleasure of it, but there was more to it than that. The truth was, he didn't believe in commitment. It didn't work. Growing up under his father's cold eye, learning not to get attached to a stepmother because each one came and went in a heartbeat...that life had taught him a lesson.

Marriage, to put it succinctly, was pointless. It didn't

work, especially if your last name was Baron. Just look at the old man, who had chalked up five wives. At Travis, who had been married and divorced quicker than a rattler could strike. At Gage, whose marriage was in trouble…

Slade drew a deep breath, then blew it out.

It was simple. Kids deserved a mother and a father and a happy home, but if you were a Baron you had as much chance of giving a kid that as a snowball had of surviving in hell. It was a truth he'd lived by and, knowing that truth, maybe even fearing it, he'd never made the mistake of planning a future that depended on commitment. Now, Lara Stevens had changed that forever.

He had a child. A son.

Didn't she think he'd want to know? And what about the boy? The kid sure as hell had the right to know he had a father.

"Slade?"

Who was Lara, to play God?

"Slade? Is that you?"

Catie. Slade closed his eyes. Catie, the Queen of Perception. She was the last person he wanted to deal with just now but there wasn't much choice. He braced his shoulders, turned and smiled.

"Yeah," he said, "it's me. What are you doing out here, away from all the fun?"

"I came looking for you." She put her hand on his arm. "You okay?"

"Sure. Just—just too much noise inside, you know? I figured I'd take a breather."

"You're a bad liar," Caitlin said gently. "Want to talk about it?"

"There's nothing to talk about, darlin'."

It was the truth. There wasn't a way in the world he was about to let anybody know what had happened, not until he knew the details. Not until he confronted Lara and maybe wrung her pretty little neck.

"Slade?"

"I'm fine," he said, and gave her the old Los Lobos salute, to make her laugh. Then he looped an arm around her shoulders, told her she owed him a dance and hustled her inside the house, back to the lights and the noise and the party.

Somehow, he made it through the rest of the evening and the next day, too. He didn't get much sleep but nobody seemed to notice his bloodshot eyes, maybe because Sunday began with Grant Landon confirming that Jonas wouldn't leave Espada to Catie even though it was the right thing to do, and ended with Natalie driving off with Landon's wife and leaving Gage behind. Travis seemed out of it, too. He went into the old man's study and came out an hour later, looking as if he'd just seen a ghost.

It was a hell of a thing, Slade thought, as he packed his suitcase Sunday afternoon, a *hell* of a thing to be relieved your brothers were too deep in their own problems to notice yours. He had to be pretty far gone, to feel that way—but not so far gone that he'd forgotten what an intelligent man could do with a charge card, a telephone and a couple of discreet calls to people who could make the right wheels turn.

His airline ticket said Boston but he flew to Baltimore. He'd phone Lara from the airport. That way, she'd have little time to prepare for their confrontation. And he wouldn't see her at her home. He wanted to meet her somewhere public, where she couldn't resort to hysterics. Not that he really thought she would; she was far too cool for that but she might try it, when she heard what she'd have to do. It was his decision, his alone. And, he thought grimly, as the plane landed, it was irrevocable.

Her phone rang several times before she picked up. She sounded as if he'd awakened her and for just a second, his mind seized on images of her in bed, all warm and sleepy. If he closed his eyes, he knew he'd be able to feel the silk of her skin, breathe in the scent of her that was all lush, sweet woman...

Warm and sweet weren't words a man could use, about Lara.

The realization strengthened his reserve. He spoke coldly, without any lead-up or niceties.

"This is Slade," he said. "Name a place where we can meet."

She said it was too late. She said she had no intention of seeing him ever again. She spoke calmly but she didn't bother asking what he wanted. She knew; he could feel it in his bones, and when, suddenly, her calmness gave way and her voice trembled, he knew she was panicked and he felt a savage sense of pleasure.

"I'm not asking you, Lara, I'm telling you. Name a place. A restaurant. A bar. I don't give a damn. Just name it, get yourself a baby-sitter and meet me in an hour." He paused, just long enough to make the next words count. "Or I'll show up at your office tomorrow morning and we'll deal with this thing publicly."

There was silence, and then he heard her take a breath.

"There's a diner," she said. Her voice trembled again as she gave him the address. This time, she made no attempt to hide her distress, and that pleased him even more.

"One hour," he said, and hung up.

Slade knew.

Lara put down the telephone. He knew. God, he knew!

What was he going to do?

Nothing. What could he do? He had no proof, just that one, quick look at Michael. As long as she stood up to him, denied everything, as long as she showed him that he couldn't intimidate her, she'd be fine.

But she had to deal with him tonight. If he came to her office and made a scene, her job would be history.

She called Mrs. Krauss. The baby-sitter was grumpy; there was probably nothing new in that but she said yes, very well, she'd come right away, for double pay and cab fare.

Lara went into the bedroom and looked down at her sleeping son. She touched his back, smoothed her hand over his soft black curls. He was hers, and there was nothing Slade could do to change that.

She threw on jeans and a T-shirt and left her house the minute Mrs. Krauss arrived.

Slade was waiting for her at a booth in the rear of the diner. The place was half-empty at this hour on a Sunday night. The waitresses were standing at the coffee machine, whispering and shooting little looks in his direction. Why wouldn't they? He was a man whose looks attracted women, made them do things they'd only fantasized.

Lara knew that, better than anyone.

He rose when she reached the booth. A matter of habit, she knew; she'd get no acts of courtesy from him tonight. He looked different, not just because of the taut set of his lips but because of the way he was dressed. She'd only seen him in suits and ties. Now he was wearing a tight black T-shirt. His biceps were prominent, as were the muscles in his forearms, and there was a ripple of muscle in his chest. He wore faded, snug jeans and scuffed cowboy boots.

He looked hard and masculine and dangerous, an outlaw of the Old West reincarnated on a hot June night on the Maryland shore.

Terror beat its heavy wings inside her breast as she slipped into the booth opposite him. She told herself to show nothing, say nothing. Let Slade do all the talking. It was her only plan.

One of the waitresses materialized beside the booth, with a mug and a pot of coffee.

"The gentleman said you'd want some."

Lara noticed the mug of black liquid in front of Slade. She nodded. "Yes, that's fine."

"Anything else? Some pie? The cherry is home—"

"Nothing," Slade said, his eyes riveted to Lara's face.

The waitress left in a rush. Lara didn't blame her. Slade was like a tightly wound spring. One touch, and he'd snap.

She wrapped her hands around the mug, letting the heat of the liquid warm her suddenly frigid hands.

"Did you really think you could fool me, Lara?"

His voice was soft and menacing. It made her want to race for the door but she looked up from her coffee and met his cold look with a little smile. "Honestly, Slade, you'd think a woman had never turned you down before. Your ego must be awfully fragile for you to—"

He slammed his fist against the table. Lara's heart jumped along with the coffee.

"Don't play games with me, dammit."

"I'm not. I'm simply saying—"

"There's nothing 'simple' about you, baby." He leaned toward her, his eyes dark and burning in his face. "Michael is my son."

Lara laughed. She tried to, anyway, but the sound she made was a pathetic bleat.

"Michael? Your son? Where did you get such a crazy—" Her breath caught as Slade grabbed her wrist. "You're hurting me."

"You're lucky I'm not beating you senseless." His hand tightened on hers. "No games, I said. He's mine. I want to hear you admit it."

"I'm not going to tell you something that's not true."

She was good. Very good. Her gaze was unflinching, her chin determined. But he could feel the telltale race of her pulse under his fingers. He eased his grip but his eyes never left hers.

"Listen to me," he said softly. "We can do this whatever way you like. The truth would be the easy way."

"I told you the truth. Michael isn't—"

"Or we can do it the hard way. Lawyers. Judges. DNA tests." He let go of her wrist. He saw the marks of his fingers before she dropped her hand into her lap and he got a funny feeling, as if he wanted to grab her hand and press his lips to the bruises but then he thought, what the hell was wrong with him? Let her feel a little of the kind of pain he was feeling. "Your choice, baby."

"Slade, listen to me. Michael isn't yours. I don't know why you'd think—"

"I don't *think,* I know! My son was born nine months to the day—to the damned day, Lara—after we slept together."

Her face paled. "You can't possibly know when Michael was born!"

"September 19." His words fell like stones between them. "Can you count backward to that night we were together, or shall I do it for you? He was born at 7:05 in the evening. He weighed seven pounds five ounces." His mouth twisted. "And when they asked the name of his father, to enter on his birth certificate, you told them to write 'Father Unknown.'" His voice roughened. "'Father Unknown,' Lara. How could you do such a thing to my son?"

Lara clasped her hands together. Her fingers were colder than ice.

"For the last time, Michael isn't your son. I told you. My husband—"

"If you had a husband, and he was the boy's father, how come his name isn't on that certificate?"

Oh, God! She stared at Slade, feeling the cold spread through her blood. Think, she told herself, think!

"It was—it was because we were in the middle of getting divorced. And—and my husband…"

"You don't have a husband. You've never had a husband. When you want a man you just go someplace and pick one up. Why limit yourself to one guy if you can screw the brains out of as many as you like?"

The crude words made her blanch but she kept her head up. "I don't have to defend my morality to you."

"No. You don't. All I give a damn about is that your story's a lie. You were never married. That ring on your finger's strictly for show."

"You can't possibly know—"

"I know everything except why you wanted to let my son grow up thinking he had no father."

"For the last time, Slade. He's not—"

"Stop lying to me!" His eyes burned into hers. "When you knew you were carrying my child, why didn't you tell me? Did you think I'd tell you to take a hike? You knew my first name, my profession, where I lived...you could have found me if you really wanted to try but okay, I'll grant that maybe you didn't know how to go about it." He took a harsh breath. "Then Dobbs handed you that file, and it was all there. Everything you needed. My address. My phone number."

"What is this, Slade? Something you lifted out of a cheap soap opera, with lots of dramatic twists and turns, and me as the villain? It's fiction. Fiction, do you understand? None of it ever happened."

"And when I showed up," he said, ignoring her protests, "you did everything you could to make me disappear."

Lara stared at him. Every instinct told her to leap to her feet and run. But she knew it would be a mistake, that the only way to face down a predator was to show no weakness.

Carefully she took a napkin from the dispenser on the table. She blotted her lips, put the napkin on the table and slid across the banquette.

"This has been very interesting," she said calmly, and wondered if he could see the pulse beating in her throat. "I mean, listening to someone's fantasies is fascinating. But it's late, and I have to get home." She rose to her feet. "Good night, Slade. With any luck at all, we'll never have the misfortune of seeing each other again."

She turned and walked toward the door, every sense attuned to the scene she'd left behind. The hard-faced man, still sitting in the booth. The cold eyes, boring holes into her spine. She waited for the sound of him coming after her but there was only silence and, gradually, her steps quickened until she was running...

He caught her just as she reached the parking lot behind

the diner. Her car keys were in her hand; she heard the pound of his feet and tried, desperately tried, to force the key into the door lock but his hands fell on her shoulders and he spun her toward him.

"Don't you want to ask me how I know so much, Sugar?" His teeth shone in a malice-filled smile. "The lies you spun about being married. The details of my son's birth."

"Let go of me! Let go, you bastard, or—"

"Michael's the bastard," Slade growled, "thanks to your deceit."

"What do you want?" The cry tore from her throat. She pulled loose from his grasp and fell back against the car.

"The truth, damn you! I have a son to claim."

She felt the blood roaring in her ears. "No. He's not—"

Slade slapped a hand against her car on either side of her, trapping her with his body. His chest, rock-hard, brushed hers. She could almost feel the waves of hot anger coming off him.

"I've already arranged for DNA tests," he said softly. "Considerin' the circumstances surroundin' his conception, and the lies you've woven ever since, I don't think I'd have any trouble suin' for—and gettin'—custody."

He'd fallen into his Texas drawl. It softened the cruel words but it emphasized his determination. He'd do it, Lara thought frantically. He'd take the matter to court, if he had to, and what chance would she have then?

The world had been reduced to this moment. To the implacable will of Slade Baron, who didn't give a damn for anybody but himself.

"What happened, baby?" He bared his teeth in a terrifying parody of a smile. "Did you forget to take your pill? Did you chicken out about getting rid of your mistake, when you realized you'd gotten yourself knocked up?"

"My son isn't a mistake. He's the love of my life, you—you son of a bitch! I wanted him. You hear that? I wanted my baby. It's the only reason I went with you that day, the only reason I let you touch me." She saw the shock in his eyes and it gave her the courage to continue. "I wanted to get pregnant, Slade. I'd thought about it for a long, long time, and I'd come up with a million ways to do it, but nothing seemed right." She drew a breath. "And then fate and a snowstorm dropped you in my path."

"Bull! You slept with me because you were as hot for me as I was for you."

It was true. She'd slept with him—made love with him—because Slade was the first man, the only man, who'd made her forget everything she knew about right and wrong. Somewhere during that long, incredible night, she'd admitted the truth to herself, that she was in his bed because of what he made her feel, not for what he could give her.

But she would never admit that to him. Not now. Not ever. It would make her far too vulnerable—and he would never believe it.

"You came along when I was at the right point in my cycle." Her voice shook, but she forced the words out so that they were cool and clear. "You were healthy, you seemed intelligent. Your looks were acceptable. And I knew, from the way you talked, that you'd be able to—to perform."

She saw what the effect her words had. He stiffened, his face hardening until it seemed all shadows and angles. He lifted his hand, curled it around her throat and she knew he was close to forgetting everything he knew about civilized behavior.

"A stud?" he said softly. "Is that what I was?"

"You're hurting me, Slade."

"Lara Stevens's private stud service."

"I wanted a baby."

"*You* wanted." He laughed, and it sent a chill down her spine. "You wanted a baby."

"Yes. I know you may not think it but I'm a good moth—"

She gasped and rose on her toes as his hand pressed harder, his thumb just in the hollow of her throat.

"And what I might have wanted didn't matter."

"It had nothing to do with you."

"Do you hear what you're saying, woman? You used me to get pregnant, gave birth to my kid and it had nothing to do with me?"

For the first time since that night, Lara felt a whisper of uncertainty. It had all seemed so right. So pragmatic. No, she thought, no, this wasn't a time to question what she'd done.

"It's not as if I wanted anything from you," she said quickly. "I still don't. Michael is mine. I carried him for nine months. I gave birth to him, I'm raising him—"

"Do you have any idea how I felt when I looked in that crib Friday night and saw my son? My son, Lara, only I was never supposed to know him, and he was never going to know me. He was going to grow up thinking his old man was some no good bastard that ran out on his mother, that left him to grow up without a father…"

"He has me," Lara said sharply. "He doesn't need a father."

"I never figured on being a father. I'd seen my family's mistakes in the marriage wars—"

"This has nothing to do with marriage. A woman doesn't have to have a husband to be a good mother."

"—I'd seen them, Lara. And I told myself, no way would I make the same mess of my life." He drew a shuddering breath. "But I thought about it sometimes, about what it might be like, to have a family. And I promised myself that if I ever did make a dumb move, get married, have kids, I'd be a good father, one my kid could love instead of—"

Bright lights lit the parking lot. Slade swung around, shading his eyes from the glare. A police car pulled up alongside them.

"Hell," he muttered, and jammed his hands into his pockets.

"Everything okay here?" An officer stepped from the car, flashlight in hand, and shone the light on Lara. "Lady? You okay?"

She swallowed dryly. "Yes. Yes, thank you, I'm fine."

"We got a call from the diner. Somebody said you didn't look too happy when you left and that this guy went after you." He swung the light and Slade blinked under its merciless glare. "You got some ID, pal?"

Slade took out his wallet and handed it over. "There's no problem, Officer. The lady and I, ah, we had a difference of opinion."

"She your wife?"

"No. She's my fiancée. We, ah, we were discussing the plans for our wedding." The policeman gave him back his wallet and Slade flashed a man-to-man grin as he pocketed it. "You know how it is. She wants all the trimmings and I just want to stand up in front of a J.P."

"Is that right, ma'am?"

Lara looked at Slade. He was smiling at her but she could see the warning in his eyes.

"Yes. It was—it was something like that."

The officer chuckled as he got back into his cruiser. "Take my advice, pal, and keep at it. Nobody in his right mind needs to go through the hoopla of a formal wedding."

"Absolutely," Slade said, and smiled—but his smile faded when he turned to Lara again as the patrol car's taillights winked, then faded into the night. "Picking me for your stud service was a bad idea."

"Look." She exhaled sharply and tucked her hands into the back pockets of her jeans. "Maybe I—maybe I shouldn't have made such a—a unilateral decision..."

Color rose in her face at his bark of harsh laughter.

"Do the words 'right' and 'wrong' have any meaning in your world, Sugar?"

"I wanted a child, Slade. And I promise you, I'll raise him with love. You don't have to worry about that. About anything. I told you, I don't want anything from you."

"You already have it. My donation to your own private sperm bank." A muscle knotted in his jaw. "That was all you wanted from me that day. Isn't that what you said?"

"I—yes. Yes, that's right."

He moved toward her. She took a step back but with the car behind her, there was no place to go.

"Why me?" She flinched as he reached out and ran the back of his hand along her cheek but though his voice was rough, his touch was gentle. "You wanted a man in your bed, you could have had your choice. How come I was the lucky sap?"

"I told you." His hand was in her hair, his fingers warm against her scalp. His breath was warm, too, almost a caress against her skin. "You were—you had the right attributes. And you were there at the right time."

He looked into her eyes. "You trembled in my arms."

"I—I don't see what this has to do with anything. Slade, please—"

"That's what you said to me when I kissed you, the first time. Please, you said, Slade, please…"

He lowered his head, slowly, slowly, even as his brain asked him what in hell he was doing. He didn't want her. She'd used him. Lied to him. She'd have gone on lying, she'd have kept him from the truth, if it hadn't been for a quirk of fate.

He paused, a whisper from her lips. Her eyes were wide and fixed on his. His thumb lay in the hollow of her throat again and he could feel the race of her heart.

"Tell me the truth," he said huskily. "That you wanted me, not just a substitute for a test tube."

He gathered her close. She was rigid but a little sound escaped her, a soft moan that filled him with triumph. He slid his hands down the length of her back, cupped her bottom and lifted her into the V of his legs, into the hardness of his arousal.

She moaned again, lifted her hands to push him away.

Instead she curled her fingers into his shirt, teetered on the brink of lunacy...

With a cry, she tore herself from his arms.

"All right." She shuddered with the enormity of the admission. "It's true. Michael is your son."

Slade bowed his head. For one heart-stopping instant, she almost reached out to touch him but she caught herself before she could do anything so foolish.

"And—I admit, I might have made a couple of poor decisions."

He looked up, his expression unreadable, his eyes cool and watchful.

"I'll see to it the birth certificate is changed." She waited for him to speak but he just went on looking at her. The silence grew unnerving. "And—and I'll tell him about you, when he's old enough to understand."

Still, Slade said nothing.

"Dammit," she said, "what more do you want?"

"You don't pay attention, Sugar, or you wouldn't need to ask. I already told you. I intend to be a father to my boy. A good father."

Lara ran the tip of her tongue over her bottom lip. Her world was falling apart, and there was nothing she could do to stop it.

"All right," she said unsteadily. "We'll arrange for—for visiting privileges. You can come to see him, I don't know, one Saturday a month—"

"Wow."

The softly spoken word oozed sarcasm. Her head came up; she balled her hands into fists. "You think it's going to be easy, giving him up to you for a Saturday?"

"I don't much care what it is, for you." He spoke calmly, which amazed him, because his heart was beating like a drum. "It's Michael who counts. I don't want our son to spend Saturdays with a man who'd basically be a stranger."

Our son. An ominous portent clung to the words but, in her desperation, Lara ignored it.

"What would you suggest, then?" Her heart skipped a beat. "I'm not going to let you take him away from me, Slade. I swear, if you try—"

"Marriage."

She stared up at him, into those unreadable eyes. "What?"

"We're going to be married. Tomorrow." His words were clipped. She thought, crazily, that he might have been arranging a dental appointment. "At noon."

She waited for him to laugh. When he didn't, she gave one bark of hysterical laughter for the both of them.

"You're crazy."

He grabbed her arm as she turned away and spun her toward him.

"It's the only solution," he said coldly. "My son is going to have two parents. A father, and a mother."

"No! I'd never agree to—"

"I'm not asking you, I'm telling you." His hand tightened on her. "And you'll be a good mother to him and a faithful wife to me or so help me, I'll take him from you." His eyes burned into hers. "If it comes to that, if he's only going to have one of us, it's going to be me. I can do it, Sugar. Don't make the mistake of thinking I can't."

It was the truth. She knew it; he could destroy her life and he would, if she didn't do what he wanted.

"I hate you," she whispered. Tears of rage rose in her eyes and streamed down her face. "I hate you, Slade. I'll always hate you—"

"Hate me," he said, clasping her face between his hands. "I don't give a damn. All I want is my son." He took a breath. "That," he whispered, "and you in my bed, at night."

"No," she said, "Slade, no," but he didn't listen. He kissed her, his mouth bruising hers. Lara groaned, at first with despair and then with self-loathing, as she gave herself up to the kiss.

CHAPTER EIGHT

Some women dreamed about their wedding day.

Lara wasn't one of them.

She'd never wasted time imagining what it would be like to be a bride. Why would she, when she knew the reality of marriage? Her father's terrifying anger. Her mother's soul-wrenching tears and blind obedience to every command he gave until one summer evening, he'd walked out the door and never returned.

Her sister was living that same life now, as if she'd never learned anything from their mother's misery. Emily was trapped in the same life that had been their mother's, worn-out and dependent on a man for her survival.

Lara had vowed none of that would ever happen to her. She'd studied hard and made herself financially independent. She'd filled her life with things she loved, travel and music and books, and when she'd felt a gnawing emptiness inside her, she'd realized it wasn't for a man—what intelligent woman would think it was?

It was for a child of her own. For Michael.

And yet, for all her clever planning, she'd made a terrible mistake.

She'd chosen Slade to be her son's father for reasons that had seemed so logical. His good looks. His obvious health. His intelligence. That he wasn't a man who'd want to hang around and stay in her life had suited her plans, and if he'd excited her in a way no man had ever done...well, that was a bonus.

How stupid she'd been.

Looks. Health. Intelligence. Sex appeal. She'd checked them all off, as if they were items on a shopping list. But

Slade had another quality, one he'd shown when he'd picked her up that day in Denver, one she'd foolishly not considered.

Slade Baron was the most determined man she'd ever met.

When he wanted something, he went after it and to hell with anything that stood in his path.

He wanted Michael. And today he'd come to lay his claim.

Lara had refused to believe it. She'd spent the night telling herself that what had happened in that parking lot had just been a man showing he was stronger than a woman...until the bell rang, at eight, and she opened the door and saw him standing on the stoop.

"You can't do this to me, Slade," were the first words out of her mouth.

"No, 'good morning, Slade.' 'Nice to see you, Slade.' Just, 'You can't do this to me, Slade.'" His tone mocked her. "I've already done it, Sugar." His words turned cold. "Dobbs is expecting us in—" he glanced at his watch "—in just a little over an hour."

"You've spoken with Mr. Dobbs?" The look on his face was all the answer Lara needed, and she felt her despair escalate into fury. "This is my life, damn you. You have no right—"

"I have every right." His eyes gaze raked over her face, paused at her lips, then lifted to meet hers. "Would you like me to prove it?"

Lara stared at him. What did the threat mean? That he'd see her in court? Or that he'd take her in his arms, as he had last night, and make a sham of her pathetic attempt at defiance?

"I hate you," she said, her voice trembling. "Do you hear me, Slade? I *hate* you! You can play your tin-god games with my life and with my son's, but you can't change the way I feel. I hate you, and I always will."

Something dark and dangerous flashed in his eyes but he

spoke with a dispassionate calmness that only frightened her more.

"Are you packed?"

"Packed? No." Lara's heartbeat fluttered. "We didn't discuss—"

"It doesn't matter." He brushed past her. "In fact, I prefer it that way."

"You prefer...?" She rushed after him as he headed toward Michael's room. "He's sleeping. Don't—"

Her breath caught. Michael was clinging to the crib rail, swaying unsteadily as he stared, round-eyed, at Slade.

"Hi there," Slade said softly. "Hi, Mike."

"His name is Michael. And he's frightened of strangers. You can't just—"

But he already had. He'd lifted Michael from the crib. And her son, her beloved, traitorous little boy, gazed solemnly into the face that was an adult version of his, and smiled.

"Hey, Mike," Slade whispered. The baby put a plump hand against his mouth and he kissed it, inhaling baby-sweet scents that were as foreign as they were welcome. He swallowed hard. There was a lump in his throat the size of a tennis ball. My son, he thought. My flesh and blood.

He turned at a muffled sound and saw Lara standing behind him, hand pressed to her lips, eyes wide and bright with tears. She looked like a woman who'd lost everything and, just for an instant, he almost felt sorry for her—but then he thought of what *he* had lost, the months without knowing he had a son, the years that would have been lost to Michael if he'd grown up without knowing he had a father, and his heart hardened.

"If there's anything here you really want," he said coldly, "get it now."

"I don't—" Her voice trembled. "I don't understand."

"And pack whatever my son will need."

"He's my son. Mine, Slade. I planned him. I gave birth to him. I've raised him without any help from you—"

"Do it. And do it quickly. We have a lot to accomplish before one o'clock."

Lara stared at him. "What?"

"The meeting with Dobbs. And, at noon, the wedding—"

"No." Lara shook her head wildly. "No!"

"—and," he said, as if she hadn't spoken, "our plane leaves at one."

"Our plane?" She wrapped her arms around herself, as if that might stop her from trembling. "Slade. Slade, listen to me. You have to be reasonable. I—I have a life here. A home—"

"Your Mrs. Krauss is waiting in a taxi downstairs. She's agreed to take care of my son while you and I see Dobbs, and then the justice of the peace."

"How do you know about her? Have you been spying on me?"

"You can list your house with a rental agent or sell it. You won't be coming back to it."

"You *have* been spying!"

"I've been collecting information, Sugar. It's easy enough to get, if you really want it."

Lara knew his barbed remark had a second meaning but she ignored it. All she cared about, all that mattered, was regaining control of her life.

"Slade, listen to me. Think about what you're doing. You're asking me to give up everything. My job. My career—"

"I'm not asking you, I'm telling you." He smiled thinly. "You want a career? Well, you have one. You're going to be a mother and a wife, and you'd damned well better do a good job at both."

She shrank back as he strode past her. Slade told himself that was fine. It was the way it should be. Hell, after what she'd done to him, she deserved everything that happened...

But the fear in her eyes, and the despair, made his heart feel heavy as he carried his son away.

* * *

At nine, Lara stood beside Slade in Edwin Dobbs's office. His arm felt like a steel clamp around her shoulders as he explained that they'd fallen deeply in love almost at first sight. She wasn't sure which seemed phonier, the smile on his face or the story he'd invented, and she waited for the Beaufort chairman to laugh.

Instead he smiled.

"I know bankers aren't supposed to admit to being romantics at heart, but I am," Dobbs said. "I must admit, though, I'm stunned."

"So are we," Slade said, tightening his arm around her. Lara knew the gesture looked affectionate but she could feel the warning bite of each finger in her flesh. "Aren't we, darling?"

Did he expect her to help him? No way. Slade had choreographed this show; let him do the dance by himself.

"And you're getting married immediately?" Dobbs laughed, shook his head in pleased disbelief. "When did all this happen?"

"Who knows the exact moment a man and woman fall in love, Edwin?" There was a smile in Slade's voice but the pressure of his arm was still unyielding. "Lara was going to tell you herself but I thought you'd appreciate hearing the news from the both of us."

"Well, that's wonderful for you, Slade," Dobbs said, as if Lara weren't there. He chuckled. "Bad news for me, though. I'm losing a fine executive."

"I'm sorry, Mr. Dobbs," Lara said. "I wish—I wish it were different."

"She means," Slade said briskly, "she wishes she could give you more notice." He looked down at her. "I'm sure Edwin understands, darling."

"If you insist," she said quickly to Dobbs, "I could stay on for a couple of weeks."

"And miss your own honeymoon?"

The chairman laughed. Slade laughed. They both looked at her as if she were feebleminded and she thought, for one awful minute, they'd chuck her under the chin, these two men busily arranging her life as if she had no stake in it.

Nonsense, Dobbs said. She was the model of efficiency. He was sure her assistant could take over with hardly a break in stride.

That seemed to sum it up. What was happening—the fact that her life was spinning out of orbit—didn't seem to matter to anybody but her. Her house was up for sale. Mrs. Krauss was earning a morning's wages. Dobbs would replace one auditor with another. Everybody was satisfied, except her, but what could a marionette do when somebody was pulling its strings?

An hour later, they stood before a justice of the peace who either believed all brides shook through the all-too-brief ceremony or simply didn't notice. Mrs. Krauss stood alongside with Michael in her arms. The ceremony took less than five minutes. At the end, when the J.P. said Slade could kiss his bride, Lara stiffened and waited for him to take her in his arms.

Whatever he might expect, she would not kiss him.

That she'd responded to him last night was a sign of weakness, and weakness could be overcome. The bottom line was that sex wasn't going to part of this farce of a marriage, not unless Slade was into rape and she was sure he wasn't. He was everything she despised, and she hated him for what he'd done to her, but she knew he was a man who'd never force a woman into his bed.

He hadn't needed force with her, eighteen months ago. And she, pathetic fool that she was, would pay for that night for the rest of her life.

But Slade didn't touch her. He didn't look at her. He thanked the J.P., shook his hand, clasped Lara's elbow in a gesture so impersonal it was meaningless and led her outside. Two limousines were waiting, one to take Mrs. Krauss to her home, one to take Lara, Slade and Michael to the airport.

Lara's heart congealed into a hard, cold lump. She grabbed Mrs. Krauss, who looked startled, and hugged her.

"Goodbye," she said, through a veil of tears. Then she stepped into the car that awaited. Slade got in with Michael in his arms. The door slammed shut behind him with an awful finality.

She'd played a dangerous game—she knew that now. She'd won Michael, but she'd lost everything else. Her pride. Her independence. Her freedom.

She wasn't Lara Stevens anymore. She was Slade Baron's bride.

They sat side by side in the first-class compartment of the jet, two strangers with nothing between them but a night of passion.

And a child.

Lara shuddered and drew her son closer in her arms. He was asleep, his dark head against her breast, his teddy bear clutched in his arm. He'd cried the first few minutes of the flight, wrenching sobs the sympathetic flight attendant said were probably the result of the change in pressure on his eardrums. It was a logical explanation and yet Lara's heart told her the baby's tears were for the life they were leaving behind, and for the unknown existence that lay ahead.

Slade had tried to soothe Michael's tears. He'd wanted to take him from her arms but Lara had clung fast.

"I'll hold him," she'd said.

His eyes had darkened and she'd waited for him to insist. But he hadn't. He'd simply opened his briefcase and pulled out a stack of papers. In minutes, she could see that he'd forgotten all about Michael.

Her mouth thinned.

She should have expected as much. It wasn't his son Slade wanted, it was victory. Now that he had it, he'd lost interest—although, just for a moment this morning, when he'd plucked Michael from his crib, she'd thought she'd seen something real and loving in the way he'd looked at the baby.

Real? Loving? From a man who made a point of ensuring she knew that what they'd done—the hours they'd shared in each other's arms—was unimportant?

Lara bit back a sob and pressed her lips to her son's head.

The only thing real about Slade was his arrogance. If he loved anybody, it was himself. He was already losing interest in Michael; with luck, disinterest would change to boredom. And then maybe, just maybe, he'd let his unwanted wife and his trophy son return to their own lives.

Lara eased her seat back, drew the baby closer and wearily shut her eyes.

Until then, she'd have to make the best of things, not for her own sake but for her son's.

Slade stared blindly at the papers strewn over his tray table and wondered what in hell he was supposed to do now.

Make the best of things, not for his sake but for his son's. Well, yeah, he'd already figured out that much. The question was, what about Lara?

Lara, his wife.

It was still almost more than he could take in. He'd flown south Friday, a guy with a dinner appointment and, after that, a weekend in Texas. Well, he'd had his dinner appointment. He'd gone to Texas. And now he was returning home with a wife and a son.

His son.

The words were still so strange. Just thinking them sent a warmth through his blood. He hadn't planned on having a child, certainly not now, maybe not ever. Having a kid was a huge responsibility, one he wasn't sure he'd been cut out to handle. It meant tying yourself to one woman for the rest of your life because, just as he'd told Lara, he'd vowed, long ago, never to repeat his father's mistakes. A man had a son, he owed the kid something. Time and respect. Love and stability. A boy had the right to know he'd come home from school each day to a mother and a father, with no changes in the cast of characters between eight in the morning and the three o'clock bell, the way there had been when he was growing up.

Then he'd taken one look at a sleepy-eyed kid and his whole world had turned upside down. And this morning, when he'd taken that kid in his arms...

Oh, hell.

He had to stop choking up like this or he'd never be able to think straight. And he had to think straight because, even if Lara thought he was a coldhearted, cold-blooded, mean-tempered son of a bitch who knew each step he was taking, it wasn't true.

In his heart, he was terrified.

What he'd done this morning was as irrevocable as it was inconceivable.

He had a wife. Her name was Lara. Other than that, he didn't know a damned thing about her. She was good in bed, yeah, but somehow, from the way she was treating him now, as if he were a cross between Count Dracula and the Frankenstein monster, he had the feeling he could forget about that part of their relationship.

Relationship? Slade smothered a groan. He had no relationship with this woman. She'd turned down the flight attendant's offer of lunch. Lobster salad, it had been, and Lara had said no. Was it because she didn't like lobster? Because she never ate lunch?

Or because she hated his guts?

He shot his wife a hooded glance. She was lying back in her seat, Michael clasped in her arms. Her eyes were closed. Was she sleeping, or was she just trying to avoid him?

So many questions, and he had no answers. But that was okay. There'd be plenty of time to learn what made her tick, assuming he wanted to bother. It wasn't really necessary. Two civilized people could live together, go through the motions of civility, pretend they didn't despise each other, all for the sake of their son...

Except, that wasn't what he wanted from Lara. He hated her for what she'd done, not just getting pregnant deliberately and then not telling him, but for all the rest. The way she'd sighed in his arms, all those months ago. Her whispers. Her caresses. The heat of her skin, the taste of her mouth... It had all been lies. It hadn't been him she'd wanted, it had been what any healthy man could have provided via a test tube.

All the things he'd remembered about making love to her were lies.

Weren't they?

She'd melted in his arms last night. God, the feel of her. The softness. He could have taken her there, in that parking lot, her against the car and him deep inside her, her mouth hot on his, his hands lifting her, holding her to him...

"Flight attendants, please prepare for our descent into Logan Airport. Ladies and gentlemen, the weather in Boston is bright and sunny..."

Bright and sunny, Slade thought, and almost laughed.

He felt Lara's seat come up straight. Michael whimpered and he turned and put out his arms. Lara stared at him.

"Give me my son," he said coldly.

He saw what little color there was drain from her face. Slowly she held the child out. He took him from her, but not before he felt the tremor in her hands.

She was afraid.

Good, he thought coldly. That was just the way he wanted her. Afraid. Terrified. Because, dammit, that was exactly what he was. Scared to within an inch of his life. The only difference was, Lara would never know it.

He'd left his car parked at the airport.

Fitting a woman, a baby, a baby seat, assorted luggage and a bag stuffed with diapers, toys, cans of juice and boxes of crackers inside his Jag wasn't easy. Lara stood holding Michael, saying nothing while he packed things away and installed the baby seat, but Slade had the feeling she was laughing at him.

Laugh, he thought grimly. Was it his fault he'd left Boston a bachelor and come back a married man with a son?

At last, they were on the highway, heading for Beacon Hill. Neither of them had spoken since he'd taken the baby from her on the plane and he was weary of the silence.

"Do you need anything?"

"My freedom," Lara said politely.

His jaw tightened, but he warned himself not to bite.

"I meant for Michael. I can stop at a shopping mall, if you like."

She looked at him. His hands gripped the wheel in a way she knew, instinctively, was uncharacteristic. He'd be a driver who would hold the wheel lightly, let the power of the car seep into his muscles and his blood as he drove it.

"I'll need a lot of things, if you're serious about keeping us here."

Slade shot her a tight smile. "Hoping I've had a change of heart, Sugar? That I'm going to turn the car around, take you back to Logan and pop you on a return flight to Baltimore?" His smile vanished. "Give it up, Lara. You're here to stay, and I'm trying to be civil. Tell me what you need and we'll stop and get it."

Lara looked away from him and focused her eyes straight ahead. The city looked gray, even on a soft summer evening. Gray and old, and alien.

"A crib," she said, and fought to keep from sounding as frightened as she suddenly felt. "A stroller. A playpen. A high chair...."

"We can buy all that tomorrow. What do you need for now?"

"Nothing, I can feed Michael on my lap, or I can improvise. When he first learned to sit, I used to prop him in the corner of the sofa, with pillows on either—" She drew a ragged breath. "I'll manage."

"What about sleeping? Will he be all right in a bed?"

She gave a disparaging laugh. "You don't know much about babies."

"No," he said coldly, "I don't."

Lara flushed and caught her bottom lip between her teeth. It had been a stupid thing to say, but she wasn't about to apologize.

"Michael will be fine. He'll sleep with me."

"For tonight."

She looked at him, at the implacable, hard profile, and felt her heartbeat quicken.

"If you think you're going to get your pleasure out of my—my servitude," she said, her voice low, "you're wrong. You forced me into this marriage but you can't force me to sleep with you."

Slade turned off the highway and into a tangle of residential streets. They were almost at their destination, and she sensed it. He could feel the tension mounting; it was like a presence seated between them. He shot a look at Lara. Her skin was pale, almost translucent, save for violet smudges of exhaustion beneath her eyes. She looked worn and frightened, and for an instant he thought of pulling to the side of the road, taking her in his arms and telling her she had nothing to fear from him, that he would take care of her and their son, that he would never ask anything else of her because theirs would not be a real marriage.

He'd said other things last night and even this morning but he'd been angry then. He was calm now, and he'd won the war. He could be generous and reassure her.

Any man would, if he had a handful of pride.

Slade pulled into the driveway of his home, hit the button for the garage-door opener, slid the Jag into place and shut off the engine. Beside him, Lara sat still as a statue.

It was just that he remembered too much.

He remembered how perfectly her breasts had filled his hands, and the way the delicate pink tips had pearled at the touch of his tongue. The sweetness of her creamy flesh against his mouth. The softness of her thighs, and the woman-scent of her arousal.

And now she'd borne his son. Had her body changed? Was it even more lushly female?

Would just the sight of her arms opening to draw him down to her still be enough to make him hard with desire and need?

The part of him that remembered the night they'd spent together hoped it would be.

The part that hated her prayed it would not.

Slade's jaw hardened. He got out of the car, went around to the passenger side and opened the door for his wife.

CHAPTER NINE

LARA came awake abruptly, heart pounding, lungs straining for breath, the demons of her nightmare snapping at her heels.

The dream had been terrifying. She'd been in a strange room, in a distant land...

It wasn't a dream. It was real. She was in a bedroom in Slade's house. Her own room, with its pale yellow walls and windows overlooking a small garden, was hundreds of miles away.

She was trapped here, trapped here with—

Lara bolted upright in the bed. "Michael?"

Fear flooded her senses. She'd fallen asleep with her arm around her baby but he wasn't there anymore. The only thing lying next to her was a teddy bear.

"Michael," she said, her voice rough with fright.

She tumbled from the bed and searched the room, got on her knees, peered under all the furniture, opened the closet and checked the bathroom.

Her baby was gone.

Frantic now, she ran to the door and flung it open. Ahead, sunshine flooded a skylight that illuminated the dangerous twists and turns of a spiral staircase.

"Michael," she whispered as her heart raced into triple-time. "Oh God, Michael..."

A peal of childish laughter rang through the silent house. Lara swung around, listening, her hand at her throat.

"Michael?" she whispered, and the sound came again, this time as a bright counterpoint to the deeper, full-throated laugh of a man. Lara ran down the hall, past closed doors,

123

following what had become giddy squeals and chortles to an open doorway at the end of the corridor…

And found Slade's bedroom, and his bed, and the source of all the laughter.

Slade lay sprawled on his back in a tangle of pale blue sheets. Michael sat on his belly, leaning back against Slade's upraised legs. They were holding hands, the man and the child, Michael's tiny fists lost within Slade's grasp.

"All aboard," Slade said, and gently tugged first Michael's left hand, then his right. *"Choo choo choo. Choo-choo-choo. Choochoochoo…"*

Michael guffawed. Laughter bubbled out of his mouth as he played with Slade. With the stranger who wanted to be his father.

Lara strode into the room. "What in hell do you think you're doing with my son?"

The giggles stopped. Michael looked around and Slade raised his head. She marched to the bed—a bed far larger than any human being needed for something so simple as sleeping—and snatched her baby into her arms.

Michael's mouth trembled. "Ma-ma-ma?"

"I'm here, sweetheart," Lara crooned, but her tone changed when she looked at Slade. He was sitting up and now she realized he was wearing nothing but a pair of white silk boxer shorts. She felt a sudden rush of heat, and that only made her more angry. "I asked you a question, Slade. Just what were you doing with my child?"

Michael whimpered and tucked his thumb into his mouth. Slade's eyes flashed a warning as he swung his legs to the carpeted floor.

"Hey, Mike," he said gently, "it's okay. Your mom was probably worried about you, that's all."

"Probably?" Lara glared at him. "I wake up and find my son missing and you think I was *probably* worried?"

"Look, I'm sorry you were upset." Slade ruffled the baby's hair. "I woke up and heard him crying. When he kept crying, I went in and got him."

"If he'd cried, I'd have heard him."

"He was crying, okay?" Slade got to his feet. "What'd you want me to do? Leave you a note?"

"You could have—" Her gaze swept over him and her face pinkened. "Do you mind?"

"Do I mind what?"

"Must you walk around like—like that?"

Slade looked down at his shorts, then at her. "These, you mean?"

"Yes." Her voice was almost as rigid as her spine. "I realize this is your house but a little decorum—"

Slade laughed. "This *is* a little decorum. I sleep in the raw but I stopped long enough this morning to put on a pair of shorts before I went to rescue my son." His gaze swept over her, taking in her sleep-ruffled hair, then skimming down the T-shirt she'd slept in. "Seems to me you're not dressed for a meeting with the Queen, either."

Her blush darkened. "I was frantic," she said. "When I couldn't find my baby—"

"Yeah," he said gruffly. "Okay. Never mind."

He swung away from her and told himself he really was going around the bend. Lace was sexy. Lace, and silk. Not T-shirts, certainly not an oversize T-shirt that had come out of his bureau drawer. She hadn't wanted to take it but she had nothing else. He'd had a couple of bad minutes during the night, lying sleepless in his bed, picturing Lara sleeping just down the hall and how she looked in that shirt.

Now, he could see what he'd only imagined. The faint outline of her nipples. The shadowed darkness at the juncture of her thighs, and the long length of her legs. She was warm and rosy from sleep, half-naked in his bedroom, and she was his wife...

Oh, hell, he thought, and he pulled a pair of jeans from his closet.

"I didn't mean to scare you," he said gruffly, as he stepped into the jeans and zipped them up. "You were asleep. I got him, I diapered him, I fed him—"

"You diapered him?"

"More or less. Don't look so amazed. I just followed the instructions on the box."

"And you fed him? How would you know what to feed a baby?"

"It was easy." Slade sauntered toward her, his fly zipped but the button on his jeans undone, his hands tucked into his back pockets. "I just asked myself what I would want, first thing in the morning. So I made Mike some crisp bacon, a mushroom and onion omelet, some home fries, black coffee…"

"What?"

The look of horror on her face made him laugh. "Relax, Sugar. I let him slop his way through some orange juice while I scrambled him an egg and made a slice of toast." He grinned at the baby, who grinned back. "And Mike ate every bit of it, didn't you, pal?"

"His name," Lara said coldly, "is Michael."

"Michael's too formal for a guy and his dad." Slade held out his arms. Lara tried to hang onto her son but he lunged for his father. "We like Mike just fine, don't we, buddy?"

She watched in silence as Slade lifted the baby high in the air. Michael squealed and kicked his arms and legs.

"Da-da," he said exuberantly.

"That's right, buddy. I'm your daddy."

"He didn't say that."

Slade looked at her and she blushed. She knew how she'd sounded, overprotective and angry, but she couldn't help it. Twenty-four hours had passed, one short day, and she was already losing her son.

"Sure he did. Mikey? Who'm I?" He held the baby up again and grinned at him. "Say, Daddy. Come on, pal. Let's hear it. Dad-dy. Dad-dy…"

"He's too young to talk," Lara said brusquely.

"He says Mama, or something that passes for it."

"He just makes sounds. Anyway, that's different. I'm his mother."

"And I'm his father," Slade said, his voice suddenly cool. "The sooner you get used to that, the better."

"You don't know anything about Michael. Not anything."

"Trust me, baby. You don't want to start down that road." Slade forced a smile to his lips. "Anyway, it worked out fine. He likes playing Choo-Choo Train, and he's partial to his old man's scrambled eggs."

"Didn't it ever occur to you to ask me what he eats?"

"I told you, you were asleep. So I called Helga."

A cold fist seemed to twist around Lara's heart. "Helga," she said brightly. "Really."

"And she said—"

"Oh, I can just imagine what she said. Caviar. Champagne. Maybe some paté…"

"Stop it."

"Don't you tell me what to—"

"I said, stop it. You're scaring the hell out of my son."

"Your son? *Your* son?" Michael began to cry. Lara glared at Slade and took the baby from him. "Now see what you've done," she snapped, and marched from the room before she could make herself look even more foolish.

She knew she'd overreacted, but she'd been worried. Couldn't Slade understand that? And, dammit, couldn't he have gotten dressed? Did he did have to stand around like that, in unbuttoned jeans with his chest bare? Did he have to display those muscled arms and shoulders? That hard chest with its silky whorl of dark hair that tapered down over his ridged belly and vanished under the waistband of the open jeans?

Lara shut the door to her room and leaned back against it while Michael snuffled against her throat.

As for whatever advice a woman named Helga might provide… Who cared?

Certainly, not she.

Her only concern was for Michael, and he was exhausted. She knew it was from the endless hours of their journey yesterday but she told herself it was because Slade had worn him out with that game.

She sang to him, rocked him in her arms. When his lashes drifted to his cheeks, she held him until she was sure he was sound asleep. Then she made him a bed on the floor, secured him within an enclosure of pillows and blankets, and blocked the open bathroom door with the chaise longue.

Showered and dressed, she carried the sleeping baby downstairs and built him another safe bed in a corner of the living room. Once she was sure he wasn't going to awaken, she followed the scent of brewing coffee to the kitchen. She knew where the room was, even without the coffee to guide her. Slade had insisted on showing her through the house last night, even though she'd made it perfectly clear she didn't give a damn what it looked like.

"I don't give a damn, either," he'd said coldly. "You can like the place, hate it—your opinion of my home isn't important. I just don't want you falling down the steps and breaking your neck, if you get up during the night."

As it turned out, she hadn't gotten up. Her sleep had been plagued by dreams but she'd slept straight through until morning, so soundly that she hadn't even heard Slade enter her bedroom.

Slade, in her bedroom, standing over her. Watching her.

The idea made her feel breathless. And that kept her anger humming.

Slade was sitting on a high-backed stool at a white marble breakfast counter, reading the paper. His hair was wet, probably from a shower, and curled lightly around his ears and the nape of his neck. He'd put on a T-shirt, thank goodness, but it was as tight and as faded as his jeans. His feet were bare, and she almost laughed because she'd half expected to see him wearing boots.

Lara frowned.

Laughter would not be helpful. Anger. Anger, was what she needed. Not laughter, and certainly not this sudden, dizzying wave of heat that swept from her breasts to her belly as she imagined coming up behind him, laying her hands on his shoulders and, when he turned, kissing his mouth.

This man—this gorgeous male specimen—was her husband.

She must have made a sound, some little murmur of self-despair, perhaps, because just as she was about to flee, Slade looked up, turned and saw her. For a heartbeat, she regretted that she'd plaited her hair into a braid, that she'd pulled on a shapeless T-shirt and a pair of old jeans she'd stuffed into a small suitcase at the last minute, but his gaze slid past her, as if she weren't really worthy of his notice, and she felt her anger return.

"I hope I'm not disturbing you," she said, with all the sarcasm she could manage.

Slade didn't seem to notice. "Not at all," he said politely. "Where's Mike?"

"Michael," she said pointedly, "is asleep."

"Is he okay alone?"

She gave him a pitying glance as she walked to the stove and poured herself some coffee.

"I wouldn't have left him, if I didn't think he was."

"There's sugar and cream, if you want."

Lara looked at him over the steam rising from her mug. "Thank you," she said coolly, "but I prefer it black."

"So do I."

"Is that supposed to make me jump up and down with joy?"

"I only meant... Look, don't you think it'll make things easier, if we know a little something about each other's habits?"

"No," she said sweetly, "not particularly."

Slade drew a deep breath, then let it out. "Okay. Okay, we'll stick to a safer topic. Tell me about Michael. I mean, I don't know much about kids—"

"Indeed."

"—but, for instance, does he generally nap in the mornings?"

"No. But he's exhausted."

"Yeah." Slade propped his elbows on the counter, wrapped his hands around his coffee mug. "Well, that was a lot of travel time we put in yesterday."

"It was this morning that tired him. All that rough play, with you."

"You think?" He grinned at her over the rim of his mug. "He loved that game I invented."

"So you may think, but he isn't used to that kind of roughhousing."

"Well, he's going to get used to it. We had a great time."

The scene she'd walked in on flashed into Lara's mind. Michael and Slade together, Michael giggling and laughing. Her throat tightened, and she gave him a pitying smile.

"Once I buy him some toys," she said, "you'll see that he prefers quieter pastimes."

It wasn't true. Her baby loved to play tickle, and I See, but none of that mattered half as much as making sure Slade understood he was an outsider. If only the man didn't have such thick skin. Right now, he looked completely nonplussed.

"Well, he'll have the chance at both. Quiet stuff, with you, and rougher stuff with me." He cleared his throat. "Speaking of toys…I got him some things."

"What are you talking about?"

"I ordered some stuff."

The words were tossed off in a manner that was loose and easy, but she could see the proud glint in his eyes.

"Stuff?" she said, cautiously. "What kind of 'stuff'?"

"Oh, some blocks. A wooden train. A couple of stuffed animals—I saw how much he loves that bear and I figured, a lamb and a dinosaur couldn't hurt."

"A dinosaur?" Lara said faintly.

"The purple one. Helga said kids love 'em."

"Helga," she said, even more faintly.

"Uh-huh. And…" He eased from the stool, folded his arms and leaned back against the counter. "And some other things. A crib. A playpen. A high chair. Oh, and a stroller...you know, stuff you mentioned yesterday."

Lara thought back to the crib and playpen, the high chair and stroller she'd had to leave behind. She thought of the pleasure she'd had, selecting them, and of how casually Slade had replaced them.

"You bought Michael all those things, without consulting me?"

"Well, yeah." His smile slipped just a little. "You were asleep, so—"

"I can see," she said tightly, folding her arms, too, "that sleeping is a mistake."

"Look, I knew Mike needed things. So I phoned Ted."

"Ted." Lara smiled stiffly. "Is that, perhaps, short for Theodora?"

"Ted Levine. My partner. He has two kids. So I asked him to give me the name of the best store in Boston to buy baby stuff." He didn't add that he hadn't told Ted the reason he needed baby furnishings. "It's info for a new neighbor," he'd said briskly, when Ted had questioned him. How could you explain, over the phone, that you had suddenly acquired a wife and a son?

"You ordered these things sight unseen, over the telephone?"

Slade's smile disappeared completely. "You don't like what I bought, you can return it, okay? I just thought—"

"Oh, I know what you thought, Slade. You figured you could lock me out of my son's life, that—that you can play with him and buy him presents and shove me into the background."

"Are you nuts?"

"Didn't you expect me to figure it out? Didn't you—"

The angry tirade caught in her throat. He was right; what she was accusing him of was crazy. Michael loved her, not the things she'd bought him. He was her baby, not something she'd won in a lottery.

Besides, how could she have an argument with a man

who looked like a bum? That damp hair. The bare feet. The tight T-shirt and faded jeans—and they were tight, too. Didn't the man own anything that didn't cling to him like a second skin? And why hadn't he shaved? She didn't like the sight of stubble on a man's jaw. Definitely, he looked like a bum.

Who did she think she was fooling? He looked sexy. Sinfully sexy, the bad boy of the girlhood dreams she'd mercifully forgotten. This was her husband, she hated him—and he was sending her pulse galloping into three-digit numbers.

"Didn't I what?" Slade said.

"Nothing. Nothing! Forget I even…" Lara puffed out a breath, counted to ten and started over. "Here's the bottom line. We're going to have to work out some ground rules."

"For what?"

"For—for everything. Just look at what's happened since I woke up this morning. You fed Michael. Played with him."

Slade threw out his arms. "Arrest me, Officer. I'm guilty."

"You bought him things—"

"And convinced the store to deliver them in—" he glanced at his watch "—in another hour." The words dripped smug self-congratulations.

"You should have consulted me," she said stiffly.

Slade hesitated, then shrugged. "Okay. I can see that."

"And then—and then there's the way you barged into my room, without knocking."

"Michael was crying."

"So you said. But, in the future—"

"In the future," Slade said softly, "it may not be necessary for me to 'barge' into your room."

Their eyes met. There was no mistaking his message. Lara started to reply, thought better of it and cleared her throat.

"And then—and then there's your reliance on the new Dr. Spock."

"Huh?"

"Dr. Spock. Otherwise known as 'Helga.'" She put her hands on her hips and smiled thinly. "To think that you turned for advice to a—a bimbo..."

"Helga? A bimbo?"

Color rose in Lara's face. "I don't care what you do, or who you do it with, but—but to ask advice from a—a Scandinavian blonde—"

"Whoa." Slade held up his hands. "Sugar, you need to get your facts straight. Helga's not a bimbo. She's not even blond. She's—"

"I am not interested in her pedigree." Lara thumped her chest with her fist. "I'm simply telling you that *I* know what my son needs and what he doesn't need. Do not, in the future, go to your—your lady friends for advice about Michael."

"Amazing," Slade said softly, "how you've leapt to so many interesting conclusions."

"You're so transparent, Slade. You think, if you wave the names of your—your harem under my nose, I'll—I'll—"

"You're jealous."

"Me, jealous of your women?" Lara laughed. "Don't be ridiculous."

"There are no 'women.' No harem." His smile was slow and sexy. "I always concentrate on one lady at a time, darlin'."

"Well, I don't care. As far as I'm concerned—"

"Maybe I didn't make myself clear, Lara. You and I are married. We're going to be good parents to our son."

"That has nothing to do with—"

"You're my wife."

"Not by choice."

"My wife," he said. He stepped away from the counter

and clasped her shoulders. "Why would I need another woman, when I have you?"

Lara's heart skipped a beat. "Let go of me, Slade."

"Why?" His gaze dropped to her lips, then lifted. "I'm not hurting you. I'm just touching you. A man's entitled to touch his wife."

"I'm not—I'm not your wife." Why was her pulse racing? Could he tell? Could he see it in her temples, in the hollow of her throat? "Just because you have a piece of paper that says we're married doesn't mean—"

"Woman," he said softly, "you talk too much."

He kissed her. It happened fast; she had no time to prepare herself for the brush of his lips against hers.

"That's what I mean," she said in a shaky voice. "Just because of that piece of paper, you think you can do whatever you—"

He kissed her again. This time, it was more than a whisper of mouth against mouth. His lips clung to hers; his hands tunneled into her hair, and he kissed her until she began to tremble.

"You want rules?" His voice was thick as honey, his eyes pools of smoke. "Okay, Sugar. Here they are. I'm going to be faithful to you. You're going to be faithful to me. No other women, no other men. You got that?"

Lara slicked the tip of her tongue across her bottom lip. "Somehow—somehow, I have a lot of difficulty, imagining you leading a celibate existence."

He smiled, and the promise in the smile turned her knees to water.

"You're a bright girl, darlin'. Surely you know the difference between fidelity and celibacy."

"Slade." Lara linked her hands around his wrists. "Let go."

"We have a lot of things to work out between us." He bent his head, kissed her again, lightly, gently, then nibbled at her bottom lip until she moaned and lifted her hands to his chest. "But if there's one place we're not going to have trouble," he murmured, "it's in bed."

"I'm not—"

"Don't lie to me, Sugar. Don't lie to yourself." He leaned back against the counter and drew her into the V of his legs. "There's never been a night in my life like the one we spent together."

Lara shut her eyes. "I don't want to talk about that night."

Slade laughed softly. "That's fine." He slid his arms around her, gathered her against him. "I don't need to talk about it, either. I just want to relive it."

"If that's the reason you insisted on this marriage, you made a mistake. I won't sleep with you, Slade. I'm not—"

"Maybe I haven't made myself clear, Sugar. This is going to be a marriage. My son—our son—is going to have a real home. He's going to have parents who love him."

"I already love Michael. But I'm not going to pretend I feel something for you when I don't."

"Love, you mean?" Slade gave a harsh laugh. "Remind me to tell you about love sometime, darlin'. About my old man, and how many times he must have had a woman purr that lie into his ear." His arms tightened around her. "Stop hating me and start thinking, Lara. We're married. We have a child we love, and better sex than most people even dream of. Be honest, admit it and we can make this thing work."

"That's a great speech but you're wasting your breath. I am not going to—"

She cried out as he spun her around and pinned her against the wall with the weight of his body. He caught her wrists in one hand, drew them high over her head.

"I may not have known you take your coffee black but I know you're a woman who needs a man's attention. That's fine. In fact, that's better than fine because I'm a man who can't do without a woman. And since there'll be no fooling around outside of this marriage, there's only one place either of us can go."

"How romantic." Lara felt tears welling in her eyes and fought them back. His words hadn't hurt her; why would they? She didn't expect him to feel anything special for her. All they'd ever had between them was sex. "You know something, Slade Baron? You're disgusting!"

"I'm honest, which is a lot more than you are."

"Honest?" She laughed. "Oh, right! You expect me to believe you'll be faithful and on the first day of our marriage, you've already been on the phone to your precious Helga."

"Helga?" Slade started to laugh, then thought better of it. He had the feeling he was ahead of the game; this was no time to try to make corrections. "Okay. You're right. Will it make you feel better if I tell you I won't, ah, I won't turn to Helga for advice anymore?"

"You could tell me you won't breathe her name anymore and it wouldn't change anything."

"Helga is nothing to me. Nothing."

"Don't lie. You couldn't wait to call her. And you couldn't wait to—to dangle her name in front of me."

"My God." Slade took a breath, exhaled it, then lowered his forehead to Lara's. "Listen, if it's all right with you, let's start over again. You come into the kitchen. I'll say good morning. You'll pour yourself a cup of coffee..."

"You boasted about Helga the second I saw you, when you were—when you were lying around in your bed half-naked, as if I could possibly give a damn about seeing you with your clothes off!"

"Will you just shut up for a while and listen?"

"I won't. I won't! You think you can have everything your way. You forced me into a marriage I didn't want, and now you tell me I'm supposed to—to amuse you in bed and to—to tolerate your lovers—"

Hell, Slade thought, a man couldn't argue with a woman with an idea caught between her teeth any more than he could argue with a horse with a burr under its tail.

"Just shut the hell up," he said, and crushed her mouth beneath his.

For a heartbeat, Lara held herself rigid in his arms. Slade didn't seem to notice. His mouth moved against hers, hot and hungry. His hands slid down her spine and curved around her bottom.

"Kiss me," he whispered, "open to me, Sugar, and let me taste you."

And, with a groan, she did.

He gave a growl of triumph, lifted her into him until she felt the hard pressure of his arousal. She gave a little cry, curled her fingers into his shirt and rose toward him.

His hands swept her T-shirt out of her jeans, moved onto her skin. His fingers were warm and rough; she shuddered with pleasure as he rode his hands up her ribs and cupped her breasts.

"You're mine now, Lara. All mine. There's no plane to catch, no way to sneak off and leave me with nothing but memories."

He pressed his lips to her throat, nipped at the flesh. Her head fell back and he licked her skin, inhaling her fragrance, drowning in her taste. She was like honey in his arms, sweet and yielding, and he couldn't wait, couldn't slow down; he had to have her now. His hands were strangely unsteady as he fumbled at the closure of her bra, and when her breasts tumbled free he shoved her shirt up, bent his head and closed his lips around her nipple. Her cry made his blood pound even more fiercely.

"Slade," she whispered, and wound her arms around his neck.

"Tell me," he said thickly, "say that you want me."

In some still-functioning part of her brain, Lara knew better than to say those words. Slade was turning her life upside down, remaking it in an image that had nothing to do with her. She didn't know him, didn't trust him, surely didn't love him...

But he was right. Something incredible happened when

they were in each other's arms. There was no denying the truth of that.

For the first time, she saw a glimmer of hope. It could work. It hadn't begun as a normal marriage but what was a "normal marriage," anyway? She'd seen what happened, when two people vowed their love forever.

Slade wanted her as his wife. He wanted Michael. He'd promised fidelity and truthfulness. And yes, she wanted him, oh, she wanted him...

"Say it, Sugar. Tell me what you want."

He kissed her again, one hand in her hair, the other at the base of her spine, kissed her until she was boneless and liquid with wanting him, and she sobbed his name and gave up the fight.

"You," she sighed, "you, Slade. I want you. I never stopped wanting you. I thought about that night a million times."

He whispered her name, undid her zipper and thrust his hand down the front of her jeans. She cried out as he found her, moved against his hand, lifted her face to his and sought the ecstasy of his mouth.

"Touch me," he said, and she did, she did what she'd longed to do ever since that time in his bed, she dropped her hand to his jeans, cupped the heat and hardness of him through the denim, moaned his name when he pulsed against her questing fingers.

"I can't wait. Lara, now. I need you, now."

He lifted her into his arms, his kiss so hot and raw she could only respond to it by sucking his tongue into her mouth, by sobbing her pleasure, by curling her arms around his neck and burying her fingers deep in his hair.

Cups, saucers, everything tumbled to the floor as he swept the counter clean with one thrust of his hand. He sat her down, their fingers merging as they pulled off his shirt.

Lara looked at him—at her husband. She touched him, traced the delicate arc of collarbone, the hard thrust of muscle in his shoulders.

"Don't." He shuddered, clasped her wrists, brought her hands to his lips and kissed them. "I don't want to come until I'm deep inside you and if you touch me, if you touch me—"

He yanked up her shirt, buried his face in the sweet hollow between her breasts. Lara moaned. Her head fell back; she dug her fingers into his hair.

"Mr. Baron?"

Lara froze. Her eyes flew open.

"Mr. Baron? Where are you, sir?"

"Slade!"

"Mmm. So delicious." He licked her. Suckled. Bit gently—

"Slade!" Lara pounded on his shoulders. "Slade, listen!"

"Lara." His hands closed on her waist, and he tugged her to the edge of the counter. "Just move forward, baby. That's my girl. Just—"

"Mr. Baron? Are you... Oh!"

The woman in the kitchen doorway stumbled to a halt, her blue eyes round as saucers in her pleasant, middle-aged face. She stared at Lara over Slade's shoulders; Lara stared back. And Michael, clutched in the woman's arms, laughed with delight.

"Oooh," he gurgled.

Lara gave a muted shriek and started to lunge from the counter. Slade grabbed her, held her still, his body blocking hers, and looked around at Helga. Then, very calmly, as if having your housekeeper and your infant son walk in on you when you were about to—when you were about to—

Holy hell.

He took a deep breath, smoothed Lara's shirt, shot a quick glance down at his fly and pasted what he hoped was a noncommittal expression on his face.

"Well," he said cheerfully, "isn't this nice? I've been hoping for the chance to make some introductions. Helga, this is Lara, my wife. And I can see you've already made the acquaintance of my son, Michael.''

If Helga had thought he was strange when he'd phoned her, a couple of hours ago, to ask her what a baby ate for breakfast, she had to think he was completely out of his head right now. He thought it remarkable that she didn't so much as blink.

"How do you do, Mrs. Baron?'' she said politely.

Michael chortled and bounced up and down in Helga's arms. "Da-da-da,'' he said.

Slade figured it was almost safe to breathe again. Lara was still as rigid as a statue under his hands, but the worst was over. Surely she could see that. He looked at her and flashed the most charming smile he could muster.

"Lara,'' he said, "I'd like you to meet Helga. My house—''

"You no-good son of a bitch,'' Lara hissed, and swung a hard right, directly at his head.

CHAPTER TEN

SLADE stood at the window in his office, gazing out at the Charles River and trying not to notice his reflection in the glass.

He had no desire to see the bruise under his eye. Even after five days, it still looked like an example of bad modern art.

Oh, yeah, he'd certainly found the way to begin married life. What could be more romantic than groping your new wife on the kitchen counter, getting caught by the house-keeper and winding up with a black eye?

"A week of cold silence," he muttered, answering his own question.

It was truly a joy, being a married man.

Gingerly he fingered the area beneath the eye. It was still tender. A grudging smile lifted one corner of his mouth. He had to admit, his wife packed one whopper of a punch.

And then, oh man, the mayhem that had followed it.

Helga's wild protestations in Finnish. Michael's guffaws, as if the scene had been staged just for laughs. Him, clapping a hand over his eye and saying, in complete disbelief, "Why in hell did you do that?" And Lara, with an economy of verbiage that he had to admit was admirable, shoving her nose to within an inch of his and saying, "You ever come near me again, Slade Baron, so help me, I'll kill you!"

She'd stalked off with the baby. Helga had stalked off on her heels. And he'd slunk up the stairs, the villain in the piece, to shower, dress and get the hell out of the house in one piece, while he still could.

Slade leaned his forehead against the cool glass. What had become of his peaceful bachelor existence? He felt as if he were living in an asylum for the mentally deranged. His housekeeper spoke to him only in monosyllables, his wife wouldn't touch the charge cards he left out for her and hadn't spoken a word to him all week. The only person happy to see him come through the door each evening was his son.

His son, Slade thought, and his lips curved into a smile.

Amazing, how fast he'd fallen head over heels for that bundle of high-paced energy all neatly wrapped in a diaper. Mike was one terrific kid. Bright. Cute. Sweet-tempered. He wanted to be one of those fathers who whipped out a walletful of baby pictures at the slightest opportunity.

First, though, he had to tell people he was married. But Tuesday morning hadn't seemed the right time to do it, not with everybody, from Jack and Ted straight through to the design assistants, showing an uncommon interest in his discolored eye.

"I walked into a door, okay?" Slade had said, before his partners could utter a word.

"Whatever you say, pal," Jack had answered, and grinned.

No, Slade thought, and sighed, it hadn't been the moment to say, guess what? I've got a wife and oh, by the way, I've also got a son.

Still, everyone at the office sensed something was wrong. He knew his mood was lousy, his temper quick, but he hadn't grasped just how bad things were until an hour ago, when he'd told Betsy she could stay on as his permanent secretary, if she wished, and she'd screwed up her face and said she'd need a couple of days to think it over.

He wasn't doing much better on the homefront, either.

"Hell," Slade muttered, as he sank into the chair behind his desk.

Except for Michael, he was a pariah in his own house. His jaw tightened. And whose fault was it?

"Lara's," he said out loud.

Certainly it was her fault. He was blameless. He'd found

out he had a son and he'd laid claim to him. What kind of sin was that? His actions had been exemplary. Okay, so maybe he'd been a little—abrupt. Heavy-handed, if you wanted to push it, but hey, what choice had there been?

"None," he said.

Not a one.

Michael deserved a family. That was why he'd had to force Lara into marriage literally overnight. Uproot her from her friends, her job, her home. Take her away from the only life she knew. It had all been necessary, if his son was to have a happy home...

Oh, hell.

Slade grabbed his jacket from the back of his chair, then hit the intercom.

"Cancel my afternoon appointments, Betsy," he said. "I'm out of here."

Helga stood at the kitchen counter, dicing carrots.

Michael sat in his high chair, waving a well-gummed biscuit and watching the proceedings with great interest.

"Da-dah," he said happily, when Slade burst through the back door.

"Hi ya, champ." Slade hoisted his son in the air, blew a noisy air-kiss against his throat. Michael giggled, Slade grinned, kissed him, then put him back into the high chair. "Hello, Helga," he said to his housekeeper's stiff back. "Where's Mrs. Baron?"

Helga took her time answering. "Upstairs." Her knife clattered rhythmically against the cutting board. "I don't think she wants to see you."

His life wasn't just a mess, it was turning into public property.

"Thank you for that bit of news," he said politely. "I appreciate the update."

Helga sniffed. Slade cleared his throat.

"So. You're getting along okay with my kid?"

Helga shot him a withering glance. "Your son is a wonderful child. He takes after his mother."

Slade nodded, as if he'd known that all along.

"Would it be possible for you to stay for the weekend?
A long weekend. Say, from this afternoon through late
Monday?"

"If Mrs. Baron needs me, I will be here."

"*I* need you here. I want to take Mrs. Baron away for a
few days." He cleared his throat again. "We, ah, we have
some problems to work out."

"Indeed."

"Well? What do you say?"

He waited, holding his breath as if Helga's answer were
the most important thing in the world. At last, she put down
the knife and turned toward him.

"I say it's an excellent idea, Mr. Baron." She wiped her
hands on her apron and lifted Michael into her arms. "And
I'd bet your son thinks so, too."

Convincing Lara wasn't quite as easy.

"I am not leaving my son," she said stonily.

"Helga will take good care of him."

"I'm sure she would, *if* I were foolish enough to agree
to spend the weekend with you, in a hotel."

He clasped her rigid shoulders, gently turned her to face
him. Her eyes were cold, her expression guarded. He
thought about how differently she'd looked at him all those
months ago, when she'd awakened in his arms, and he wondered, suddenly, what would have happened if he hadn't
launched into that dumb kiss-off speech, if he'd said, instead, Lara, I want to see you again. Finding you, making
love with you, has been—has been—

Slade frowned. "You have the wrong idea," he said
gruffly. "I'm not asking you to spend the weekend in bed."

A faint wash of pink dusted her cheeks but her gaze was
unflinching. "No?"

"No." He let go of her, stuffed his hands into his trouser

pockets. "The thing is—the thing is, I'm beginning to think I handled this wrong."

Lara eyed him with caution. "What does that mean?"

"It means maybe I, ah, maybe I should have done things differently."

For the first time in days, her mouth softened. A smile eased across it and Slade felt his heart lift in response. He hadn't realized how miserable he'd felt, seeing hatred in his wife's beautiful eyes.

"Are you serious?"

"Yes."

"Oh, Slade." She smiled, really smiled, and his heart didn't just lift, it soared. "Slade, thank you."

He smiled back at her. "You're welcome."

"It won't take me a minute to get ready." She spun away from him, pulled open the closet door. "I don't have very much to pack."

His smile dipped. "I know. I never even gave you the chance to get your things together. That's why I left you those charge cards. You should have—"

"No. I didn't want to take anything from you." She looked at him again. "You won't regret this," she said softly. "I promise."

He nodded, not trusting himself to speak. "I'm sure I won't."

Lara dumped an armload of things on the bed. "I'm sure Beaufort will take me back. I might even be able to get my house again but if I can't, I'll send you our new address and phone number, and—"

Slade caught her arm and dragged her around so she faced him. "What?"

"Our address. Michael's and mine." Lara smiled. "I have a confession to make, too."

"Do you," he said, his voice flat.

"I was wrong, about Michael not needing you. I can see how much it means to him to have you around." Her smile was brilliant. "You can visit him every weekend, if you

like. All you ever have to do is phone and tell me—'' She
gasped as Slade's hands dug into her flesh. "What's wrong?
Why are you looking at me that way?''

"Amazing," he said softly, "how quickly I forgot how
cold and manipulative you can be.''

Lara's smile faded. "I don't understand.''

"No, you sure as hell don't.'' He let go of her, because,
all at once, he didn't trust himself to touch her. He was
more angry than he'd ever been in his life. Did she really
think he'd let Michael go?

Did she think he'd let her go? a voice inside him whispered, and that only made him more angry.

"I'm not dissolving our marriage.''

Her face fell. "But—but you said—''

"I said, maybe I moved too fast. Maybe I should have
given you a few days to adjust to the idea of becoming my
wife.''

"No.'' The clothes she'd been holding slipped from her
hands and fell to the floor. "No, Slade.''

"Yes, Slade,'' he said, with derision. "That's what I
came to tell you, that I could see I'd made a mistake in
timing. I want Michael to grow up in a home, not an armed
camp. And that's what this house has been, ever since I
brought you here.''

Lara stared at him. "I must be missing something. You
made a mistake in timing. And you think you're going to
solve the problem by checking us into a hotel for the weekend?'' She laughed in a way that made his gut clench. "You
must think I'm an idiot!''

"We're going to spend the weekend getting to know each
other, my adoring wife, and settling our differences so we
can come home and be decent parents to our son.''

"Oh, sure. A little music, a little candlelight—''

"I hate to disappoint you, Sugar, but seduction isn't part
of my plan.''

"That's it. *Your* plan.'' Lara's voice rose as he strode

from the room. "Your plan. Your son. Your life. You think you own the world!"

"I own you," he said, turning toward her. The tightly banked fury in his eyes made her catch her breath. "And don't you forget it."

"Never," she said, in a voice filled with venom. "Never, never..." Her words trailed off to a whisper as Slade vanished from sight. "Never," she said brokenly, and buried her face in her hands.

Why did she make him so angry?

Slade gritted his teeth.

Every time he tried to talk sense, Lara twisted his words, tossed them back in his face and he ended up saying things he didn't mean. He didn't own her. He couldn't imagine any man "owning" her. She was too fiercely independent for that.

He scowled and stepped harder on the gas, even though the Blazer was already flying.

If he had half a brain, he'd have let her continue her packing. Goodbye and good riddance, he should have said. Just leave my son here and you go on and get out of my life. The only reason he hadn't done it was because Mike deserved a mother and father. That was why he tolerated his wife's attitude.

He shot a glance across the console. Lara was sitting as far from him as she could get. Well, that was fine. To think she'd figured he was taking her away to seduce her... That was a laugh. She was his kid's mother. Period. End of story. He had no more desire to take her to bed than he had to— to walk on the moon.

What man would want to make love to a wildcat? To take her in his arms, caress her skin. Kiss his way down her body, lick her breasts, her thighs. Open her with his mouth, part her petals as if she were a flower, then kneel between her thighs, lace his fingers through hers and watch her eyes darken with pleasure as he slid deep, deep inside her...

Slade bit back a groan, shifted in his seat and forced his concentration onto the road. If only she'd say something, at least ask where they were going…

But she hadn't said a word since she'd come down the stairs, her expression stony, and marched out to the car. He sighed. It was, he thought unhappily, not a good beginning to the weekend.

Dammit, what was going on in that head of hers?

Dammit, Lara thought, what was going on in Slade's head?

He was probably waiting for her to ask him where they were going. Let him wait. She'd burst before she put the question to him.

She thought about it, though, as the miles ticked away. Where *were* they going? They were flying along the road in a black Blazer—her first clue that he hadn't booked them into a Boston hotel. Well then, she'd figured, they were going to Cape Cod…but the turnoff for the Cape was long behind them. Now, even the elegant inns and handsome bed-and-breakfasts that dotted the Massachusetts shoreline were only memories.

And still, Slade didn't speak.

Lara shot a surreptitious glance at him from under her lashes. Of course, he didn't speak. How could he, when he'd been chiseled in granite? That hard profile, made even harder by the tight-lipped set of his mouth and the defiant angle of his jaw…

Go on, she thought, sit there like a statue.

It didn't matter to her how angry he was. Letting her get her hopes up like that. Letting her think he was freeing her from this ridiculous marriage. Lara frowned, folded her arms and hunched deeper into her seat. Why was he so stubborn? This marriage couldn't work; didn't he see that? Michael wouldn't have a very happy home if his mother and father despised each other.

There was no sense in pointing that out, though. She

knew that. Slade Baron wasn't just arrogant and self-centered, he was stubborn as a mule.

He was also the most gorgeous man in the world. And one heck of a terrific kisser.

Lara blinked and sat up straight. Where had *that* silly thought come from? So he kissed well. Who cared? So he knew how to touch her until she trembled. Who cared about things like that? The only reason he'd gotten so far the other morning was—it was—

It was because she'd wanted him to do it. To do everything. Kiss her mouth. Her throat. Her breasts. She'd wanted him to touch her, to take her, right there on the kitchen counter.

Crazy. Crazy, that's what it was. She'd never wanted to do anything like that, never even thought about it. It was just a good thing Helga had walked in. If she hadn't—if she hadn't...

Heat swept through Lara's blood. She turned her face to the window, and blanked her mind to thought just as Slade turned off the highway, onto a country road.

They were in Maine, now; a sign a while back had said so. The road narrowed, began climbing. At dusk, he pulled to a jarring stop outside a sagging wooden structure. He switched off the engine, got out of the car and came around to where Lara sat, arms folded, eyes straight ahead.

"Are you getting out?" he said brusquely.

She looked past him to the lopsided building, then back at the road. "I'd rather sleep in the car."

"You'd have to," he said dryly. He opened her door. "This is the general store. You want to have something to eat while I buy supplies, fine. You want to sit here and sulk, that's fine, too."

Lara glared at Slade. He glared back.

"Suit yourself."

He was gone for a long time. She sat stiffly in the car, listening to her stomach growl and giving up the idea of a hotel once and for all. Where was he taking her? She'd be damned if she'd ask, not even when he finally reappeared with an enormous box in his arms.

He put the box in the back of the Blazer, then got behind the wheel and dumped a small package in her lap. Lara looked at it as if it might be alive.

"What," she said with disdain, "is that?"

"A roast beef sandwich." He glanced at her as he pulled onto the road. "It wasn't my idea, believe me. Ernie—he owns the place—Ernie spotted you sitting in the car like a martyr—"

"I am not a martyr. I simply want nothing from you."

"Yeah, well, it's not from me but if you don't want the sandwich, hand it over. There's never been a time since I started coming up here I'd pass up Ernie's roast beef."

Lara looked at Slade. Started coming up where? she wanted to say. Instead she unwrapped the little package, lifted the crusty roll to her lips and took a bite. The snap of horseradish mayonnaise filled her mouth and her stomach almost groaned with gratitude.

"Good?" he said, when she was down to the last bite.

"It's okay." She looked at the crumbs that were all that remained of the sandwich, licked her fingers and shrugged. Why not admit it? He hadn't made the sandwich, he hadn't even bought it for her. "Very good."

He nodded and concentrated on the ever-narrowing road. It was better than thinking about the way she'd put her fingers between her lips and sucked each one clean.

The way his wife had sucked her fingers clean.

A shudder rocketed through him. He stepped down on the gas, and the car shot ahead.

The trees grew taller, the encroaching forest more dense. Lara had given up all hope of figuring out where they were going. The only thing she was sure of was that no self-respecting hotel would be found in such surroundings. The sun set; stars glittered like jewels caught in the treetops, and still they traveled on.

Finally, when she was beginning to think they were going

to drive straight off the edge of the earth, Slade turned down a narrow dirt road that opened into a clearing. His headlights picked out a cabin that looked to be made of as much glass as wood. He shut off the lights, then the engine. Silence, as deep as the forest, closed around the car.

"This is it," he said.

This is what? Lara thought. There was only the house, the night, the woods…and the man seated beside her. This stranger who was her husband.

Suddenly it was hard to breathe.

"Where…" She swallowed, then cleared her throat. "Where are we?"

"Lake Arrowpoint." He jerked his head toward the cabin. "I built this place a couple of years ago."

Slade cleared his throat, too. His voice sounded strained, although he couldn't imagine why it should. He certainly hadn't used it much during the last few hours. He got out of the car, went around to Lara's door, opened it and held out his hand but she ignored it, stepped from the car and brushed past him. The dismissiveness of the gesture angered him, probably more than it should have, but there was something decidedly unpleasant about being treated like an unwelcome annoyance by your own wife.

"The ground's uneven," he said, trying for a neutral tone. "And there's some give in that bottom step. I've been meaning to fix it but—"

"I'm really not interested."

Her words were so curt they were almost cruel. Slade knotted his hands into fists as he watched her climb the stairs to the porch. Her posture was rigid and unforgiving, and suddenly he imagined the three days that lay ahead and how it would be, just the two of them in this isolated place with nothing but their mutual dislike for company.

He'd been foolish to bring her here. Hell, he thought, as he unloaded the groceries and their carry-alls from the car, he'd been worse than foolish. He'd been stupid. They had things to discuss, yeah, but they could do that someplace else. How could he have made such a misjudgment? He'd never brought a woman here before. He'd known better. A man came to a spot like this with a woman, she had to be special. Someone he wanted to be alone with, not just for a night but for days. For weeks, maybe for the rest of his life...

"Are you going to unlock the door or am I supposed to stand out here all night?"

Lara glared down at Slade from the porch. The moon had risen and she could just make out the look on his face, something halfway between anger and disdain and she thought it was exactly the way she'd look, if someone took that petulant tone with her.

It was just that she couldn't help it.

How dare he bring her to this place? How *dare* he? A cabin in the middle of no place, isolated, cut off from the world. Would there be running water? Telephones? Electricity? Would there be anything to do for the next few days except suffer Slade's unwanted company?

She turned her back to him, her head high, and jammed her hands into the pockets of her jeans.

He wanted to talk? Okay. Okay, fine. They could talk in Boston. In New York. They could talk in the middle of the damned street, anywhere, anyplace...but not here. Not in this peaceful, quiet spot where there'd be nothing to look at but Slade, nothing to think about but Slade, nothing to do but wonder how it would feel if Slade loved her, if he'd brought her here because he wanted them to spend the next days and nights in each other's arms...

Lara swung away from the door.

"Take me back to the city!"

"Don't be ridiculous."

"Did you hear me, Slade?" She put her hands on her hips and glared at him as he trotted up the steps. "I don't want to stay in this—this godforsaken place."

"It's late," he said brusquely, as he unlocked the door and stepped inside the dark cabin. "You're tired and irritable and so am I. You'll see things differently in the morning.''

"I'll see them just the same as I do now. Listen to me! I do not want to stay here. Is that clear enough, or do you want me to say it again?"

Instead of answering, he dumped their bags inside the door and fumbled for the switch. Light blazed on, illuminating a room she knew she might have admired if she hadn't been so furious. The walls were made of hand-finished logs; the floor was planked. A long, low sofa stood before a massive fieldstone fireplace.

"I heard you." Slade put a hand in the small of her back, propelled her forward and shouldered the door closed. "And I'm just heartbroken that you don't care for the accommodations."

Lara swung toward him, her face pale except for two bright spots of color high on her cheeks. "What did you expect, Slade? That one look at your—your deep woods hideaway and I'd decide you weren't such a bad guy after all?" Her chin lifted; her blue eyes snapped with defiance. "I don't like you. You don't like me. And all the talking in the world, about Michael, about our differences, won't change that."

Slade watched her move past him and reach for the door. He could feel something building inside him, a tidal wave of rage that had nothing to do with what she'd said or even with what she'd done to turn his life inside out. It had to do with what had been in the back of his mind for days, and it was time he dealt with it.

"You're right." His voice was low and rough. "Talking about our son isn't going to help."

"Honesty, at last," Lara said.

Maybe it was the way she said it, in a voice touched with contempt. Maybe it was the way she turned her back to him and reached for the doorknob, as if she were a queen and he were a subject she'd dismissed. Whatever it was, Slade snapped. A growl burst from his throat. He grabbed her by the shoulder, spun her toward him and pushed her back against the wall.

"You want honesty, Sugar? Honesty's what you're gonna get."

Lara looked up into Slade's face. His eyes were the flat gray of thunderclouds before a storm; his mouth might have been chiseled from granite. Fear fluttered its wings in her belly.

"Let go of me," she said quietly.

"Did you ever stop to think that I'm no happier about this than you are? That maybe I had plans for my life, too, and the last thing I wanted was a wife to screw things up?"

"I'm not the one who insisted on this joke of a marriage!"

"No. No, you sure as hell aren't." His mouth twisted. She made a move as if to try to slip loose and he jerked her back into place. "As far as you're concerned, Michael doesn't need a father."

"I told you, I changed my mind about that. I said you could visit him as often as you liked, if you just let me out of this marriage."

"If I just let you go running back to Baltimore, you mean."

"It's my home. It's where my job is. Where my job was, until you came along and decided to play God. Didn't you care that I had a life there? A home? A career? Friends?"

"Friends," he growled, and the way he said the word put all her senses on alert.

"What," she said carefully, "is that supposed to mean?"

"Men friends. That's what you're talking about, baby. A woman like you doesn't have any other kind."

"You don't know anything about a woman like me."

"I know all I need to." His smile was feral. "Or am I supposed to forget how we met?"

"I don't believe this," Lara said, with an incredulous laugh. "*You* picked me up, remember?" She poked a finger into his chest. "*You* asked me to go to that hotel. And *you* were the one who went out of your way to make it clear all you were interested in was that one night…and now you're acting as if I was some sort of—of immoral seductress?''

"You picked me out of the herd, Sugar, like you were a mare in heat.''

"A mistake I'm evidently expected to pay for the rest of my life.''

"How many times had you done that before, huh?'' Slade clasped her jaw, tilted her head up and held it fast. "Come on to a guy, wiggle that pretty little behind and bat those thick lashes and make him think you're offerin' him a piece of heaven when all you want from him is to get laid. How many men were there before me?'' His mouth twisted. "A dozen? A hundred?''

Lara stared up into Slade's furious face. For one crazy minute, she wondered what would happen if she told him that the wild sexual history he'd created for her was so far from the truth it was laughable, that she was a woman who never so much as kissed a man on a first date…

"Too many to count?'' he said, and anger mixed with hurt made her lift her chin, look him straight in the eye and give credence to his accusations with a lie.

"That's right. Far, far too many to count.''

Slade's eyes went black and he smiled like a wolf baring its fangs.

"I see. Well, we're making progress, at least.'' His hands slid into her hair. She'd braided it and secured it with a clip but one rough tug and she felt it come undone. "The lady's decided to be truthful.''

"Look, there's no point to this. You've admitted we made a mistake by coming here. Let's just get back into the car and—''

"How many after?''

"I don't understand.''

"Come on, Sugar. You're a smart girl.'' He moved closer to her, until his body brushed hers. "How many men have you been with since me?''

None. The word begged for release and yet she held it back, knowing he wouldn't believe her and knowing, as well, that it would be dangerous to give him that information.

"None of your business."

He laughed softly, tilted her face up to his, bent his head and brought his lips to within a whisper of hers. Her heart kicked in her chest. Something terrible was going to happen; she knew it. The air had turned thick; the night was supernaturally still. All she could hear was the beat of her own heart.

"Of course it's my business, considerin' that you're my wife."

Lara tried to pull away but it was useless. Slade was almost leaning against her now, his body touching hers everywhere from her breasts to her thighs. Heat swept through her blood as she felt him, hard and erect against her belly.

"Don't," she whispered.

"Don't what? Ask you about all the men you've slept with?" He bent his head, gently bit her neck. She closed her eyes, held back a moan. "Okay. I won't. You're right. They're the past." His voice roughened. "Unless there's somebody you left behind, in Baltimore."

"Slade. Slade please, don't do this..."

"Is there?" He moved, shifted his weight, caught her wrists and drew her hands out to the sides so that she was helpless. Vulnerable—vulnerable, and, oh God, suffused with desire. For him. Only for him. "Just tell me that, damn you. Was there a man when I took you away?"

What was the right answer? What would protect her, not from his anger because she knew, even now, that he wouldn't hurt her. Not physically. What she needed was protection from her own feelings...

"Tell me," he said, and before she could find an answer, he kissed her.

His mouth was hard on hers and when she cried out and tried to turn her head away, he let go of her hands and clasped her face, holding her imprisoned for his kiss. She struggled, tried to tear free, but he was relentless, his mouth and hands taking what he needed...

What she needed.

She didn't want to fight him, or herself. She wanted Slade. She wanted her husband. She loved him, she couldn't lie to herself anymore. She knew now that she'd loved him from the beginning, but she could never tell him that. If she did, his power over her would be complete. He would truly own her, body and soul.

She could only give herself to him, and be taken by him. It wasn't enough, but it was all she could have.

Tears rose in her eyes and spilled down her cheeks. "Slade," she whispered, her voice trembling, and she lifted herself to him, wound her arms around his neck and opened her mouth to his. "Make love to me, Slade. Please, make love to me now."

Slade drew back and looked down into Lara's upturned face. She was weeping, but the smile that curved her lips filled his heart with happiness.

"Yes," he said, only the one word but it was enough. Then he lifted his wife into his arms and carried her through the cabin, to their bed.

CHAPTER ELEVEN

IT WAS a wide bed, with soft pillows, and as Slade brought Lara to it, he thought how right it was that he should make love to her here for the first time since they'd married. He'd never brought a woman to this place, or this bed. It held no memories, no past. There was only the future, and what he and she would make of it.

He put her down beside the bed and began to undress her, pausing to kiss each bit of skin as he uncovered it. Moonlight stretched a pale finger through the windows and touched Lara's face with the softest ivory hue.

Slade lowered his head and pressed kisses along the trail of moonlight until his mouth found hers.

"You're so beautiful," he said softly, and when she smiled against his lips, he drew her close and touched the tip of his tongue to hers.

Her clothing fell away under the brush of his fingers, baring her body to his mouth and his hands. He was taut with the need to take her, to bury himself inside her, but everything had gone too fast between them from the day they'd met.

This time—this time, he would savor each moment.

He dipped his head, kissed Lara's throat. Her head fell back and he felt her pulse race against his lips.

Slowly, he told himself again, go slowly. She was his and the night had only just begun.

But he could feel his urgency growing, feel the blood thundering through his veins. She was so lovely, his wife. So perfect, standing before him dressed, at last, in nothing but moonlight. He cupped her breasts and felt their exquisite weight against his callused palms, watched her face when he brushed his thumbs across the rosy tips.

"Oh," she whispered, "oh, Slade..."

"Do you like that?" he said thickly, and she moaned and slid her hands under his T-shirt, her fingers cool against his fevered skin.

He bent his head, kissed her nipples, teased them with his teeth and tongue. Her knees buckled and he swept her into his arms and laid her on the bed.

"Now," she said shakily, "now, please..."

He came down beside her, stopped the breathless plea with a kiss and traced the lush contours of her naked body with his hand. The softness of her breast. The feminine curve of her hip. The slight convexity of her belly and then, at last, the hot, wet heart of her.

The sound she made when he touched her there was almost his undoing.

My wife, he kept thinking, this is my wife.

She was everything a man could dream of, and more. And she was kissing him, touching him, holding him as if he were all *her* dreams come true, as if were the only man who'd ever mattered.

God, if only it were so.

Stop thinking, he told himself furiously. Just feel. It wouldn't matter how many men there'd been, not after tonight. From now on, she would belong only to him. She would dream of him, as he'd dreamed of her for the last eighteen months. She'd whisper his name in the darkness. And when he took her in his arms, she'd look into his eyes and she'd say—she'd say—

Slade drew back and stripped off his clothing. Lara lifted her arms, sighed his name and he came down to her and kissed her again and again, each kiss hungrier, deeper, more passionate than the last.

"Now," she said, her mouth trembling against his, "please, Slade, now."

He moved over her, knelt between her thighs. He took

her hands in his, their fingers laced tightly together, and drew them out to the sides. He shifted his weight and she moaned when the tip of his engorged member brushed her labia. Her hips lifted, her body arched like a bow, but still he held back.

"Look at me," he said roughly. She opened her eyes. They were black and deep with need, and he fought to hold his hunger in check. "Now say my name," he whispered. "Say it, as I come into you."

"Slade," she said, her voice breaking, "Slade, my husband, Slade..."

Slade groaned, pressed forward and lost himself in the softly yielding body of his wife.

It was late. Very late, somewhere in the darkest hours of the night. The moon had set but dawn had yet to touch the eastern sky.

Lara lay with her head on Slade's shoulder, her hand splayed across his chest, and thought how lucky she was, to have found this man...this man who was now her husband.

He had made love to her with wild passion and then with such sweet tenderness that she'd wept in his arms. Then he'd drawn her close against him and she'd tumbled into sleep, still safe and protected in the warm confine of his embrace.

Lara sighed, turned her face against Slade's shoulder and brushed a soft kiss against his skin.

She'd been such a fool, fighting against this marriage, thinking that Michael was all she needed to complete her life. Her child was the joy of her existence and always would be, but Slade—Slade was the blood, flowing in her veins. He was the warmth of her soul, the beat of her heart...

Oh, how she loved him. She knew that now, without question. She'd loved him since that first moment he'd walked into her life, all those months ago, and now—now, she was even willing to hope there might come a day she could tell him she did.

The time would have to be right. Saying "I love you" to a man who didn't love you could be a burden instead of a blessing, even if the man were your husband. Slade had married her because of Michael. He'd brought her here to convince her that they could work things out and make a good life together, that they could deal with each other with civility and certainly find pleasure in bed, but that didn't mean he wanted to hear her say, Slade, I've fallen in love with you.

It would be so sweet to say it, though. To lean over her sleeping husband, wake him with a slow, gentle kiss, to smile into his eyes when he opened them and say...

"Sugar?"

Slade's middle-of-the-night voice was husky and soft. Lara smiled as he lifted her hand from his chest and kissed it.

"Hi," she said softly. "I'm sorry if I woke you."

"Don't be." He turned onto his side, brought her against him and kissed her mouth. "I was dreaming about you."

"A good dream?"

"A wonderful dream, darlin'...but what's a dream compared to wakin' up and findin' you right here, in my arms?"

He kissed her again and rolled her beneath him. She looped her arms around his neck. His body was warm against hers, and excitingly aroused, and already she could feel the thickening of her blood as he moved against her.

"Mmm. That feels—oh, that feels—"

"That's how it feels to me, too," he whispered, and moved again.

"You can't. I mean, how could you? Not so soon. Not after... Oh."

"Oh, indeed, Mrs. Baron."

Lara gave a soft, sexy laugh. "I guess that's one of the benefits of marrying a younger man."

"A younger man, huh?"

"Didn't you see it on our marriage license? I'm two years older than you are."

Slade chuckled. "My birthday's next Friday. So for a little while, anyway, there won't be such a huge gap in our— Hey!" He laughed while she struggled in mock fury. "I like older women."

"You do, huh?"

"Sure." She felt him smile against her throat. "It takes so little to make them happy. For instance..."

Lara wanted to tease him, to say she had no idea what he meant. But he kissed his way slowly down her body, lingering over her breasts, her thighs, tasting her essence, then moving up over her and entering her, slowly, slowly, rocking against her...

And she was lost to the night, to the world, lost to everything but him.

The first blush of dawn light woke Slade from a sound sleep—that, and the sounds of mice in the kitchen.

That was his first thought, anyway, as he lay listening to the faint clink of metal and glass. A couple of field mice had come wandering in when he'd first built the cabin, but mice didn't cook bacon, he thought, as he sniffed the air. They didn't play the radio or sing, either. And if they did, he doubted it would be in such a soft, sexy alto.

He pulled on his jeans, zipped them up. Barefoot, he made his way silently through the house, to the kitchen, and paused in the doorway.

Lara was standing at the counter, her back to him. Coffee dripped through the filter into the glass carafe; as he watched, she forked crisp strips of bacon from a skillet onto a paper-towel-covered platter. The griddle was heating on the stove, and a bowl of what he hoped was pancake batter stood waiting alongside.

Slade grinned, folded his arms and leaned back against the door frame. His wife had a domestic streak. That was nice to know. She was bustling from refrigerator to sink to stove with an efficiency he hadn't expected—and boogying to an old Elton John tune, while she did. Her hips and backside were in gentle motion.

And what a sweet backside it was.

He suspected she wouldn't like knowing he was watching her. She might even haul off and try to slug him again but it was a risk worth taking. A man would have to be a saint not to want to hang around a while and admire the view. Lara, with her strawberry-blond hair streaming over her shoulders, wearing his discarded T-shirt and her lace panties...

This was ridiculous. He was watching his wife and getting turned on and—

Lara swung around, saw him and shrieked.

"Hey." Slade held up his hands. "I didn't mean to scare you." He laughed at the look on her face, walked across the room, cupped her elbows and lifted her to her toes for a slow, thorough kiss. "Good mornin', darlin'."

Lara smiled. "Good morning. Breakfast is almost ready."

Slade reached past her and stole a strip of bacon from the platter. "Mmm. Crisp. Just the way I like it. And is that pancake batter I see?"

"It is," she said, turning to the stove. "You do like pancakes, don't you?"

Slade grinned and hitched a hip onto the edge of the counter. "Show me a Baron who doesn't, and I'll show you an imposter."

Lara smiled and began pouring batter onto the griddle. "How many of you are there? Barons, I mean."

"Well, let's see. There's the old man—Jonas, our father. And there's Travis and Gage, my brothers. And our stepsister, Caitlin, although she's really not a Baron..." He paused, and his voice softened. "You'll like them all, Sugar, even my old man. And they'll like you."

"I hope so," she said, with a nervous laugh. "Have you told them yet? About us?"

"No. Not yet. My brothers have been having some problems of their own. And everything happened so fast with you and me…'' Slade reached for another strip of bacon. He didn't want to talk about the unpleasant circumstances of their marriage, especially now, after the night they'd shared. "How about you? Have you told anyone?"

Lara flipped a row of pancakes. "No." Her voice was so low he had to strain to hear it. "There's only my mother and my sister. And—and I'm not close with either of them."

"Oh," he said, and waited for her to say more, but she didn't. He tried to imagine not feeling close to Trav or Gage but it was impossible. "So, uh, where do they live?"

"Outside Atlanta." Lara began stacking pancakes on two plates. "My mother's on her third husband. Or maybe he's her live-in. I'm not sure. All I know is that he treats her like dirt. My sister's married." She looked up, her eyes suddenly bright with defiance. "Her husband treats her the same way."

"Hey." Slade eased off the counter edge. "Lara, darlin'…"

She brushed past him and put the plates on the table. "Breakfast is ready. Let's eat before it gets—"

"Lara."

He felt her shudder as he took her in his arms. She stood rigidly within his embrace and he knew she wanted him to let her go but he didn't. He couldn't, not once he'd glimpsed the pain she carried. Instead he gentled her as he would a spooked filly, running his hands lightly up and down her back, letting his warmth surround her. After a long time, she put her arms around his waist and buried her face in his neck.

"I'm sorry," she whispered.

"Don't be." He pressed a kiss into her hair. "Would it help to talk about it?"

She never did, never had. It wasn't that she was ashamed of her mother…well, maybe she was, just a little. But if she told Slade about her, and how hard she'd worked not to repeat her life, he might understand…

"Sugar?"

Lara looked up at her husband and wondered if her mother had ever felt this way. It didn't seem possible but perhaps her mother had once loved her father, almost as much as she loved Slade. Maybe she'd put her trust in her husband, the way she was tempted to put her trust in Slade.

Love, and trust. That was what it took, to make a marriage.

Lara shuddered, and Slade's arms tightened around her. "Darlin', what is it?"

"Nothing," she said, "it's nothing."

"Lara."

She looked up. The look on his face was so serious that she was almost afraid to hear what he was going to say.

"My childhood wasn't exactly *Happy Days*, either," he said. His voice was gruff but his touch was gentle as he stroked her hair back from her face. "You and I are going to do a lot better than that for our son." He put his hand under her chin and lifted her face to his, his heart catching when he saw the glimmer of tears on her cheeks. "And for each other, darlin'. I promise."

Lara shook her head. She wanted to tell him not to make promises because promises were painfully easy to break but he bent to her, before she could speak, and kissed her.

"Breakfast can wait," he said softly. "Come with me, Lara. Let me show you the best way to greet the morning, and to begin the rest of our lives together."

The rest of our lives together. The words sang in Lara's heart.

"How?" she whispered.

Slade swept her into his arms and kissed her. She sighed and buried her face in his neck as he carried her back to their bed.

The weekend ended far too soon, but it led into a wonderful week.

By Friday, Slade felt like an old married man.

The thought made him grin.

Slade Baron, husband and father. Who would have believed it?

He was happy, he thought, as he put his signature to a stack of letters Betsy had brought in a few minutes before. Happy? That was the wrong word. Of course he was happy. What man wouldn't be, if he had a gorgeous, passionate wife and a son who was obviously going to grow up to be a rocket scientist or a star pitcher for the Red Sox or maybe an architect who would outshine even his old man?

Slade's grin widened.

What he was, was complete. Yes, that was it. For the first time in his thirty years—his almost thirty years, he thought, glancing at his desk calendar—for the very first time in his entire life, he felt whole. He had a wife and a son, and they had closed a circle he hadn't even realized needed closing.

It was time to break the news to Trav and Gage and Catie. And to his partners, who'd already figured something was up because, as Jack had put it just yesterday, he kept walking around looking like a cat with an endless supply of canaries in cream sauce. Well, he would tell them, all of them—right after this weekend.

It was going to be a very special weekend.

He suspected Lara was going to give him a birthday present. She had that look about her the last couple of days, the one that said she knew something he didn't. He smiled. He might be in for a surprise but she was, too. He was going to tell his wife she'd already given him the most precious gifts in the world. First Michael, and now herself. She was the best thing that had ever happened to him. He wanted to tell her that, in a very special setting.

It was the reason he was leaving early and heading home, unannounced.

Slade slipped on his jacket and picked up the letters. Whistling softly, he strolled from his office, dropped the letters on Betsy's desk, wished her a pleasant weekend and headed to the street.

Last weekend had been wonderful. He and Lara had walked in the woods, and fished. Well, he'd fished. Lara couldn't bear the thought of putting a worm on a hook so she'd simply sat beside him, dangling her feet in the cool lake water. Later, he'd cleaned the trout he'd caught and cooked them over the grill on the deck, and then he'd enticed Lara into stripping down to the buff and going skinny-dipping. They'd made love in the water, and then he'd carried her back to the cabin and they'd made love again.

Slade grinned. "Control yourself, Baron," he murmured, as he got behind the wheel of the Jaguar.

It had been a great weekend, but this one was going to be even better.

That was why he was heading home two hours early. He'd made all his plans days ago. First he would fly them to New York in his Comanche. He'd stay low, out of the way of the big planes, so she could see how beautiful the city was, from the sky. That view had always made his skin prickle, and he wanted to share it with her.

Then they'd take a taxi to the Plaza, where he'd booked a suite overlooking the park. They had dinner reservations at a French restaurant Ted Levine said served the best pot-au-feu this side of the Atlantic and afterward, he'd take her dancing, then finish the evening with a carriage ride through Central Park. And first thing tomorrow morning, he was taking his wife to Tiffany's. A woman should have an engagement ring and a wedding band, even if her husband gave them to her after the fact.

He'd give her a weekend to remember, tell her what she meant to him...

And try not to wonder how many other men had done the same stupid thing.

"Hell," Slade said. He pulled the car to the curb, oblivious to the sudden angry blast of horns behind him.

Why did he keep thinking that way? It didn't matter how many men there'd been before him. What counted was that there'd never be another man after him. He'd made it clear that he expected Lara to be faithful and besides, they made each other happy. She wouldn't look elsewhere. She wouldn't need to.

"Damned right, she won't," he said, and headed into traffic again.

He entered the house through the back door. Helga was at the sink. She looked up in surprise and he put his finger to his lips.

"Upstairs," she whispered, and he smiled and eased past her.

That meant Lara was in their bedroom. Their bedroom, he thought, as he went toward it. After last weekend, neither of them had even suggested sleeping alone. Amazing, how his life had gone from disaster to paradise in so few days.

He paused in the open doorway, smiling as he caught sight of his wife. She was sitting on the edge of their bed, her back to him, talking on the telephone in a low-pitched voice.

"No," she said, and gave a soft, husky laugh, "no, he doesn't suspect a thing."

Slade felt the smile freezing on his lips. He told himself to make some noise. Clear his throat, shuffle his feet—do something, anything, to let her know he was listening...

"There's no way he can find out, not if I don't tell him, and believe me, I won't. Uh-huh. Yes, I know. Lots and lots of champagne." She laughed again, the sound low and intimate. He could see that she'd crossed her legs and was swinging one foot, back and forth, back and forth. "I'm willing to leave the details up to you. I know, I know; we don't know each other very well but... Fine. I'll meet you there. Yes, in the suite. At seven. Well, maybe a bit later, if I can't come up with an excuse my husband will buy. Me, too. I can't tell you how much I'm looking forward to tomorrow night, Elliot. Uh-huh. Yes. Goodbye."

Slade could feel his blood pounding in his ears. He watched as Lara hung up the phone, sighed and lazily stretched her arms over her head.

In that moment, he hated her as he'd never hated another human being in his life. It was all a lie. Everything. The things she whispered, when they made love. The way she looked at him, as if he were the center of her universe.

He wanted to go to her, sling her over his shoulder, carry her down the stairs and throw her out of his house. Or maybe shove her back on that bed, rip off her clothes and unzip his fly and take her even as she fought him off, just take her again and again until she knew goddamned well who she belonged to...

He must have done something, made a sound, because suddenly she looked around.

"Slade." She bit her lip and rose to her feet and, damn her, she couldn't even control the gleam of guilt that shone in her eyes. "Slade, you're home early."

He said nothing. What could he say, while his wife tried to smile?

"How long have you been standing there?" He could see her throat constrict as she swallowed. "I mean—"

"I know what you mean," he said, his voice a monotone, barely above a whisper. He shoved his hands deep into his trouser pockets because he was afraid of what he might do with them otherwise. "I know exactly what you mean, Lara."

She smiled nervously, tucked a strand of hair behind her ear and came toward him. "Did you, ah, did you over-hear...?"

The towering wave of fury that threatened to drag him under must have shown on his face because she took a hurried step back when he moved. Not in time, though. He caught her by the shoulders, his hands hard on her flesh but not nearly as hard as the pain he could feel gutting his heart.

"Who is he?" he said. "Who's the man you're planning to meet?"

Her mouth dropped open. "What?"

"The man. The son of a bitch on the phone." He shook her and her hair flew around her face. "Tell me his name!"

"There is no man." Lara's voice trembled. "There's only you."

Slade let go of her. He wanted to believe her. God, he wanted to.

"You don't trust me," she said.

"How can I? You lie as easily as most people breathe." He caught hold of her again, anguish darkening his eyes. "Tell me who you were talking to."

Lara stared into her husband's face. She could tell him, and bare her heart to him, but what was the sense? He might pretend to believe her but the same thing would happen, again and again. Sooner or later, Slade would strip her of everything. Her pride. Her dignity. And perhaps, even, her love. It took love and trust to make a marriage, she thought, just as she'd thought it days before, at the cabin...and Slade wasn't capable of either, when they involved her.

The realization was shattering, but he would never know it. The only thing left to her now was her pride.

"No," she said softly, and pulled free of his grasp.

His face twisted. He raised his hand and she waited, head high, for a blow that never came. Instead he swung away from her and pounded his fist into and straight through the wall. He felt her brush past him, heard the clatter of her footsteps on the steps, but he didn't move.

It was over. His dreams of what might have been, his hopes—everything was finished. He had a wife and a son but nothing else because he knew the truth, now, the truth he'd worked so hard to deny.

His wife was everything he'd thought she was, the embodiment of every female who'd plagued the Baron clan. She was immoral. Deceitful. Unfaithful.

And he, Heaven help him, had fallen in love with her.

CHAPTER TWELVE

DAYLIGHT faded, became dusk. Dusk gave way to nightfall, but Slade hardly notiood.

Lara was gone. She'd left in a cab, an hour ago, and she'd taken Michael with her. He'd watched from the window—watched, and let it happen because he knew now that the world he'd created had been a fantasy. He'd wanted his son to have two parents and a loving home but a man couldn't orchestrate that any more than he could tell the wind which way to blow.

His heart ached with the loss. Not of Lara—hell, he'd known what she was when he married her. He didn't love her. A couple of hours sitting here, in the darkening room, and he'd shaken that foolish illusion out of his head.

It was Michael he was going to miss. Slade's jaw tightened. If Lara thought she was going to keep him out of his son's life, she was wrong. Tomorrow morning, first thing, he'd phone his attorney, tell him to begin whatever proceedings were necessary to gain custody.

No. Dammit, he couldn't do that. Slade scrubbed his hands over his eyes. The boy loved his mother and she loved him. And whatever else she was, Lara was a good mother. Joint custody, then. He'd have his son weekends, holidays, summers…let his lawyer work it out.

That was what he should have done, right from the beginning, instead of forcing Lara into marrying him. What a damn-fool thing that had been to do! You designed a building, you could count on it turning out the way you'd intended, but you couldn't build a family by design. One man, one woman, one child didn't add up to anything, without love. It wasn't enough that he loved his son. A marriage wasn't a marriage without love.

And he had never loved Lara. He'd known that, going in. He'd wanted her, yes. She was incredible in bed but there wasn't anything else between them...

The phone rang. Slade grabbed it. "Hello," he snarled, "and whoever this is, I'll tell you right now, I'm not in the mood for chit-chat."

"Well, neither am I," Travis snarled back.

"Trav?" Slade sat on the edge of the bed. "Hey, man. How'd you know I needed to—"

"What the hell is the matter with the female of the species, kid?"

"The fact that they *are* female. That's what's the matter with them."

"Yeah." Travis cleared his throat. "The thing is—there's this woman."

"There always is."

"I asked her to move in with me."

Slade got to his feet. "You what? Listen, before you do anything serious—"

"It isn't serious. I mean, okay, it's serious now. But it won't be serious forever. We have an understanding. We stay together, no strings, no commitments—"

Slade made a choked sound he hoped might pass for a laugh. "They all want commitments. But they want them when they want them, not when you get around to making them."

"Huh? What are you talking about?"

"Nothing. Nothing at all. Look, about this babe—"

"She's not a 'babe.' Her name is Alexandra."

"Alexandra." Slade rubbed the back of his neck and told himself to concentrate on what Travis was saying. "Classy name. Wasn't the babe—the woman who bought you at that auction named Alexandra?"

"What if she was?"

"Hey, there's no need to get defensive. I'm just surprised, that's all. I mean, the lady bought you for hot times—"

"Watch how you talk about her," Travis said coldly.

"All I'm saying is that it's sort of unusual that she's become your mistress."

"She's not my mistress."

"What would you call her, then? If she's living in your house?"

"That's the problem. She's got to be called something when I introduce her to people."

"She has a name, right? So just use it."

"We're living together, dammit. How do I let people know that?"

I have a wife who hates me, Slade thought. How do I let people know *that*?

"Well?" Travis said. "You got an answer for me, kid?"

Slade didn't have answers for either of them, but he figured that wasn't what his brother wanted to hear.

"Well," he said slowly, "why should they have to know it?"

"Because she doesn't want to be some kind of secret, as if she doesn't have a real place in my life." Travis sighed. "I just need to call her something."

"Your date?"

"Hell, no."

"Your lover?"

"No, she'd never go for that."

"How about calling her your friend?"

Travis laughed, and Slade closed his eyes. You could always do what I did, he almost said, you could marry her and call her your wife...

"She's your mistress," he said brusquely. "Leave it at that."

"She's not. Well, okay, she is. The thing is, she's more than a mistress."

"Then tell her so," Slade said, trying to curb his impatience. His brother was tied up in knots because he had a woman living with him but dammit, she wasn't his wife. She hadn't walked out the door because he was too dumb or maybe too proud to tell her how he really felt, that he— that he—

"Yeah," Travis said, "maybe you're right. 'Princess,' I could say, 'Alex, I just want you to know that you're more than a mistress to me...'"

The line went dead. Slade looked at the phone, thought about calling Travis back, then thought better of it. His brother, asking him for advice about a woman? Hell, that was a good one. He didn't know a thing about the species. Just look at what he'd been thinking, a minute ago, that maybe he'd—he'd felt something for Lara.

Okay, so making love with her was fantastic. And he liked being with her. Talking to her about stuff, nothing special, just things he'd never discussed with another woman. He'd told her about the redtail hawks that nested in the old oak near the cabin. About how he'd built that cabin himself, log by log. He'd even told her about that first week tending bar years ago, when he'd put himself through school, and how he'd managed to spill a Scotch and soda in the lap of the head of his department.

And Lara had listened as if every word was wonderful and exciting, and he'd listened to her the same way, smiling when she told him how much in common they had, how she'd worked her way through school as a waitress and dumped tomato soup all over her first customer.

Slade groaned and ran his hands through his hair.

Who was he trying to kid? Yes, he missed Michael but losing his wife was like losing his soul. He'd see his son again, smile with him, hug him, kiss him, share his life, but Lara was lost to him forever. Her smile. Her sweet laughter. The way she looked, first thing in the morning, her face shining with joy as he gathered her into his arms and kissed her...

The telephone rang again. Slade grabbed it, his heart racing. Maybe it was Lara...

But it wasn't. It was Travis, calling back.

"Listen, kid," he said abruptly, "Gage just phoned. He's having a bad time."

"Yeah," Slade said. "There's a lot of that going around lately."

"Just call him, okay? I'll give you his number."

"I know his number."

"He isn't home. I got this from my caller ID box. Take it down."

Slade scribbled the numerals on a pad, then rubbed his forehead. "Listen, man, actually—actually, this isn't the best—"

"Tell him not to be an idiot," Travis said, gruffly. "No man should ever let a woman he loves get away from him."

"Love," Slade said, and laughed again. "Who even knows what the word means?"

"You'll know, kid. Believe me, when it happens, you'll know."

Travis hung up. Slade sighed and dialed the number his brother had given him. It wasn't a good night for the Baron brothers.

Gage answered immediately. "Slade? How'd you—"

"Travis called me."

"How? I didn't give him this number."

"Welcome to the age of the chip," Slade said dryly. "His caller ID box gave it to him. Where are you, anyway?"

"Palm Beach, and don't ask, okay? It's a long story."

"Listen, man, I just called to tell you Travis is right. Whatever you do, don't let Natalie get away from you."

Gage sighed. "You know, for a couple of freewheeling bachelors, you guys sure are full of advice for the lovelorn."

"You love a woman," Slade said roughly, "you're a fool if you ever let her walk out of your life. Understand?"

"Aren't you the guy who's watched legions of broads march into the sunset?"

"Legions don't count for a damn," Slade said. "It's just one woman, *the* woman, who matters. A man finds her, he should have his head examined, if he lets her get away. You got that?''

"I've got it. But you're the last one I'd expect—"

"Tell me about it," Slade said, and hung up the phone. Slowly he walked to the window and looked out at the dark street. Lara would be at the airport by now, waiting for the plane that would take her back to Baltimore.

The plane that would take her out of his life, forever.

"Hell," he whispered.

Gage was right. Who was he, to give anybody advice about love? He didn't know a damned thing about it... except, he did. Maybe the Lara he'd loved was nothing but illusion but he had loved her. He'd go on loving her for the rest of his life. The memories of her—of how she'd slept wrapped in his arms each night, of the smile that lit her face each evening as he came through the door—those would fill his lonely nights but they weren't enough. He wanted her. Lara. Warm, and real, and in his arms...

"Mr. Baron?"

Slade looked up. Helga was standing in the doorway. Her tone was polite but the look on her face said he was the last person on earth she wanted to deal with. Welcome to the club, he thought, and gave her a tight smile.

"What is it, Helga?"

"I wondered if you'd want dinner, sir. It's getting late, and—"

"No." He turned his back to her and stuffed his hands into his pockets. "No dinner, thank you."

"I'm sorry about..." She cleared her throat. "Mrs. Baron said she wouldn't be back."

"That's right."

"Well, then...would you want me to call Mr. Elliott for her, sir?"

Slade shut his eyes. He could hear Lara's voice, the sexy laugh, the way she'd purred, *"He doesn't suspect a thing..."*

"Sir?"

"No," he said, very calmly, "that's all right, Helga. Why don't you just give me his address and I'll—I'll deal with Elliott."

Helga nodded. She dug a business card from her apron pocket, and gave it to Slade. He read it and frowned.

"Elliott and Stefan?" He looked at his housekeeper. "Catering à La Carte?"

"Yes, sir." Helga licked her lips. "Stefan is my nephew. That was why I recommended them to Mrs. Baron."

"I don't—I'm not following this, Helga. You introduced my wife to—to—"

"I suppose it can't do any harm to let you know about it now, sir. The party she was planning, I mean." Helga knotted her hands together. "Well, I don't think you'd call dinner for two a party, but Stefan said he and Elliott would be happy to handle it. Elliott—such a nice man, sir—Elliott knows the manager of the hotel, you see, and he said he could—"

"The hotel," Slade said, trying not to grab Helga and shake the story out of her more quickly.

"The one where your wi—where Mrs. Baron booked the suite. For tomorrow night. For your birthday? Oh, she took such care, sir. She asked me the name of your favorite champagne and was there any special dish you... Mr. Baron? Are you all right?"

"No," Slade said in an unsteady voice, "no, I'm not all right. I've got a block of wood where I'm supposed to have a brain, and..."

Why was he wasting time, talking? Slade hurried across the room, paused just long enough to give a shocked Helga a hug and a kiss and raced down the stairs.

He called every airline he could think of on his car phone, on the way to the airport. None would tell him if a Lara Stevens or a Lara Baron had purchased a ticket for a flight to Baltimore.

"Security restrictions," one clerk finally said, when Slade roared out his frustration.

But he learned that only one line had a flight to Baltimore leaving within the next hour. He had no choice but to hope Lara was booked on it.

He didn't even bother trying to find a parking space. Instead he pulled to the curb in front of the departure terminal for East Coast Air.

"Hey," a voice shouted, "you can't leave your car there…"

Slade didn't look back. He ran. He felt as if he were running not just to catch the plane before it left but for his life. Time was slipping through his fingers. What a fool he'd been, not to have told his wife what he should have told her days ago, what he'd tell her now…

If she'd listen.

God, she had to listen.

He raced through the terminal, checking gate numbers as he went, slowing only when he reached the security checkpoint because he knew damned well he'd never get past it if he shouldered the woman ahead of him out of the way. A lunatic was on the loose, the guards would figure, and they'd be right. Only a crazy man would have shut Lara out of his life…and only a crazy man wouldn't have realized she loved him as much as he loved her, and that he could trust her, forever, with his heart.

The way she'd slept in his arms, ever since that night at the lake. The way she'd given herself to him each time they made love. Why had he been so blind? He knew women and yes, he knew sex. And what they'd done together hadn't been sex, it had been something more: it had been a way of saying "I love you" without words.

Where was she? This was the right gate, the right waiting area. So many people. He couldn't see her. Couldn't find her. Couldn't…

Slade's heartbeat stumbled.

There she was. His wife. His beautiful, beloved wife. She was standing at the window, staring out at the night, with Michael, asleep, in her arms.

He took a deep breath and thought of all the times in his life when he'd known that what he said next might change the future. The first time he'd stood up to his old man. The time he'd talked his way into college, and then into grad school. Turning points in his life, all of them…but nothing, compared to this.

If he lost Lara, he lost everything.

Slowly he started toward her, trying feverishly to work out what he'd say. I made a terrible mistake. Can you forgive me? Will you give me another chance?

But when she swung toward him, as if she'd sensed his presence, and he saw the anguish in her eyes, his apology flew out of his head.

"Lara." His voice broke. "Lara, I love you. I need you. I can't imagine my life without you. I was wrong about everything. Sugar, I'm sorry. I'm so terribly sorry I hurt you…"

His words stumbled to a halt. He'd lost her. He could see it in the way she just stood there, looking at him, her eyes empty of everything but pain.

A cold hand seemed to tighten around his heart.

"I love you," he said softly. "I've loved you all along, ever since that day in Denver. Do you remember? You thought I was just another guy, hitting on you, and maybe I was—but then I kissed you and I was lost."

He paused, waiting for her to speak, but she was still silent. Slade took a deep, deep breath.

"I was afraid to admit it, even to myself. I didn't believe in love, Sugar. I thought it was because of my father, and what I'd seen, growin' up. I was afraid of how defenseless I'd be, if I ever gave away my heart." His mouth curved into a rueful smile. "What I never figured was that I'd meet a woman who'd take my heart, whether I was ready to give it or not." His smile faded. "Darlin', please. Tell me you'll give me another chance. Tell me you'll come home with me, that you'll let me spend my life provin' my love to you."

"You broke my heart tonight," Lara said softly.

Slade clasped her shoulders. Between them, their son sighed in his sleep. "I know I did, darlin'. If I could go back, undo all that—"

"I was planning a surprise for your birthday." Her voice trembled. Tears rose in her eyes and turned them into glittering stars. "And then you walked in, and I was so happy to see you, and then you said—you said—"

"I was wrong, Sugar. I know there's nobody else for you, the same as there's nobody else for me."

"There never was." Lara looked at him through a spill of tears. "I'm not what you thought, Slade. There's no long line of men in my past. As for what I did in Denver, agreeing to go that hotel with you—"

"It was my doin', sweetheart. I know that. I'm the one who talked you into it. I seduced you."

"I wanted you to."

Her smile was tremulous and teary, but he felt his heart leap with hope.

"Did you?" he said softly.

Lara nodded. "And it wasn't because..." She looked down at their sleeping son, then up at Slade. "It wasn't because I wanted a child. Oh, I did, I wanted a baby...but I went with you because of what I felt for you, Slade. I'd never felt that with another man, the sense that I'd—that I'd found a part of myself that had been missing, that now I would be—"

"Complete."

"Yes. Complete."

They stood looking into each other's eyes. After a long moment, Slade clasped Lara's face in his hands. He smoothed his thumbs along her cheeks, stroking away her tears.

"I love you. My heart and my soul are yours. And I want you to marry me."

Lara gave a watery laugh. "Aren't you forgetting something, Mr. Baron? A license? A justice of the peace? A ceremony that took place almost two weeks ago?"

"That doesn't count. We did it for all the wrong reasons." He smiled. "I want you to marry me again, Sugar, this time for all the *right* reasons. Because we love each other, and because our lives won't be complete without each other." His eyes searched hers. "Will you say yes?"

Lara didn't hesitate. "Yes," she whispered, "oh, Slade, yes."

He kissed her, his mouth gentle on hers.

"We'll do the thing right, darlin'. At Espada, with my whole family lookin' on. Me in a tux, you in a white gown and a veil."

"It sounds wonderful. But you don't have to do this." Lara lifted her hand and lay it against his cheek. "That ceremony in Baltimore—"

"It was legal." He grinned, and for the first time in hours, she could see the mischief dancing in his eyes. "Which means, my beautiful wife, that I don't intend to let you out of any of your matrimonial obligations, just 'cause we're gonna do this thing up right in a few weeks."

Lara grinned back at him. "Amazing, how that accent of yours just comes and goes."

They smiled at each other and then their smiles faded. Slade reached out and took Michael gently from Lara. He clasped his son in one arm and put the other around his wife.

"Let's go home," he said softly.

Tears of joy blurred Lara's eyes. She rose on her toes and pressed a kiss to her husband's lips.

"Yes," she said. "Let's."

EPILOGUE

THERE had never been a wedding at Espada before.

Marta Baron smiled at her reflection in the mirror as she applied the last touches to her makeup and thought how remarkable it was that things could so quickly change.

Just a little more than a month ago, her stepsons had come home to the ranch under duress. They hadn't said so—they were fine young men and wouldn't have wanted her to know how little they enjoyed returning to Espada—but Marta knew how they felt. And each had been troubled, as well.

She smiled again.

Now, on this brilliant summer afternoon, the house rang with their laughter, as well it should. There was nothing more joyous than a wedding. She said as much to Jonas, when he came up behind her and looked at her in the mirror.

"Isn't it lovely, having such a wonderful celebration at Espada?"

Jonas nodded. "You and Catie did one heck of a job, all right." He took something from his pocket. "Got a little somethin' for you," he said, and looped a diamond-and-emerald choker around his wife's throat.

Marta smiled and lay her hand over his. "It's beautiful, Jonas. Thank you."

"Goes real nice with that there gown."

"Yes, it does. Good. I want to look just right. I've never been the stepmother of the groom before."

"You don't look like nobody's stepmother, gorgeous. Why, you don't hardly look old enough to be my wife."

Marta turned around. "And you don't look old enough to be the father of three married men," she said as she tied his bow tie.

Jonas chuckled. "Flatterer."

"Well, it's true." She sighed, gave a last pat to his tie and smiled up at him. "What a happy day this is! Gage and Natalie, back together again—"

"And Natalie with a bun in the oven."

Marta rolled her eyes. "Such a delicate way of putting it, darling, but yes, it's lovely that she's pregnant. And Travis, with a wife—"

"And Slade with not just a bride but a son." Jonas looked past Marta, into the mirror, and smoothed back his hair. "Baby came a little early but what the heck, he's a good-looking little guy. Got all the best Baron attributes."

"They're nice girls, Lara and Alexandra. You'd think the two of them, and Natalie, had known each other all their lives." Marta sighed. "Now, if Caitlin would just find a good man, and my daughters, too."

"Hell's bells, woman, you got one weddin' about to take place and here you are, already plannin' more. Give 'em time, why don't you? It'll happen." Jonas turned her to face him. "Now, gimme a kiss, tell me again how I don't look a day over sixty, and then let's go down and greet our guests."

Marta smiled, rose on her toes and wound her slender arms around her husband's neck.

"You don't look a day over thirty," she whispered, and pressed her mouth to his.

Slade stared into the mirror in his old bedroom.

"How do I look?" he said, for the tenth time.

Gage and Travis looked at each other and tried not to laugh.

"Handsome as sin," Travis said solemnly.

"Perfect," Gage said, just as solemnly.

"No, I'm serious. You don't think this collar's too tight? Or that this tie—"

"You look wonderful," Catie said, peeping into the room around the half-opened door. "Can I come in?"

"And me?" Alexandra said, carrying Michael and following behind Caitlin.

"Me, too," Natalie said, and went straight into Gage's welcoming arms.

Travis smiled at Alex, thought how amazing it was that she'd married him, and drew her into a quiet corner.

"Nice," he said softly.

She smiled back at him. "You, too, cowboy. I haven't seen you in a tux in quite a while."

They both smiled at the shared memory of their first meeting and then Travis cleared his throat.

"Actually," he said, "it's the, uh, the accessory I was referring to."

"The what?"

"The accessory." He smiled and touched the baby's nose with his finger. Michael giggled, grabbed his uncle's hand and dragged it into his mouth. "I was thinking... I was thinking how nice it might be if we had a baby."

"Were you?" Alex blushed. "That's good. That you were thinking it, I mean. Because I was thinking it, too."

Travis bent his head and kissed his wife tenderly. "Sweetheart," he whispered.

"Darling Travis..."

"Oh, yuck," Caitlin said, laughing as she snatched her nephew from her sister-in-law's arms. "Come on, Mikey. Let's go find us a corner where everybody isn't standing around being sappy."

She carried the baby out into the garden and took him from guest to guest, smiling as he gurgled and enthralled them all. A little while later, when the chamber orchestra on the lowest level of the waterfall deck began playing, she followed her musical cue and fell into the wedding processional along with both her sisters-in-law.

At the altar, still holding Michael in her arms, surrounded now by her stepbrothers and Marta and Jonas, she felt a catch in her throat when she saw the look on Slade's face as he watched Lara come toward him, radiant in a long, full gown of white lace, her strawberry-blond hair crowned by a coronet of white flowers.

After the ceremony ended and the wedding party had gone on to mingle with the guests, Caitlin put her mouth to Michael's ear.

"You see, sweetie?" she whispered. "Your daddy and your mommy love each other so much that it makes me feel good just to look at them. It's the same for your uncles and aunts." Caitlin's voice shook, ever so slightly. "They're all happy, Mikey, because that's what love does for some people. It makes them happy."

"Brrrp," Michael said, and blew a bubble.

"I agree with you, sweetie. Love—that man and woman stuff—is okay for them but it's not for us. It's just silly. The land. This land. That's all that matters."

"Catie?"

She looked up. "Slade," she said brightly. She kissed him, kissed her new sister-in-law and handed Michael to his father. "It was a beautiful ceremony, you two. Just beautiful."

"Catie," Slade said, "what's wrong?"

"Yeah," a chorus of male voices said. Travis, Gage and Jonas surrounded the little group. "What's the matter with you, girl?" Jonas said gruffly. "Don't tell me you're blubberin' over the sight of two people givin' up their freedom, the way all these other darned-fool women are doin'."

Caitlin shook her head. "It's the sun. It's so bright, it just made my eyes tear, that's all. I'm going to—to get a tissue..."

She rushed away before anyone could stop her.

"Now, what in blazes do you suppose that was all about?" Jonas said to his sons.

"Espada," Gage said. Everyone looked at him. "Don't look at me as if I'm nuts. She was talking to the baby and I overheard her." He shot a pointed look at Jonas. "She loves this place, and she knows it'll never be hers."

Travis nodded. "Gage is right. That's why Catie's upset, Father."

Jonas frowned. "I know that, dammit. I jes' wish the girl was my own flesh and blood."

Slade put his arm around Lara's waist and drew her away. "Let them argue," he said, and smiled at her. "I don't give a hoot. Not today." He kissed his son, riding in the crook of his arm, then kissed his bride. "I'm the happiest man alive, Mrs. Baron."

Lara lay her head against her husband's shoulder. "And I'm the happiest woman." After a moment, she sighed. "It's not Espada."

"What's not Espada?"

"The reason your stepsister was crying."

Slade lifted an eyebrow. "What is it, then?"

"She needs someone," she said softly. "Someone to make her complete."

Slade frowned. "Little Catie?"

Lara smiled. "Little Catie," she said, and kissed Slade who was, and always would be, her heart and her soul.

HARLEQUIN PRESENTS®

Seduction
SWEET REVENGE

They wanted to get even. Instead they got...married!

by bestselling author

Penny Jordan

Don't miss Penny Jordan's latest enthralling miniseries
about four special women. Kelly, Anna, Beth and Dee
share a bond of friendship and a burning desire to
avenge a wrong. But in their quest for revenge, they
each discover an even stronger emotion.
Love.

Look out for all four books in Harlequin Presents®:

November 1999
THE MISTRESS ASSIGNMENT

December 1999
LOVER BY DECEPTION

January 2000
A TREACHEROUS SEDUCTION

February 2000
THE MARRIAGE RESOLUTION

Available at your favorite retail outlet.

HARLEQUIN®
Makes any time special ™

Look us up on-line at: http://www.romance.net

HPSRS

Looking For More Romance?

Visit Romance.net

HARLEQUIN ⬥ PRESENTS®

Passion™

Looking for stories that **sizzle?**

Wanting a read that has
a little extra **spice?**

Harlequin Presents® is thrilled to bring
you romances that turn up the **heat!**

In November 1999 there's *The Revenge Affair*
by Susan Napier, Harlequin Presents® #2062

Every other month there'll be a
PRESENTS PASSION book by one of your
favorite authors.

And in January 2000 look out for
One Night with his Wife by Lynne Graham,
Harlequin Presents® #2073

*Pick up a PRESENTS PASSION—
where seduction is guaranteed!*

Available wherever Harlequin books are sold.

HARLEQUIN®
Makes any time special ™

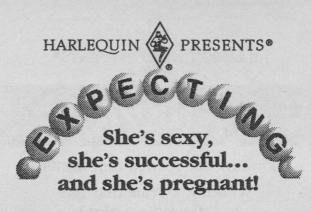

Coming Next Month

#2067 A CONVENIENT BRIDEGROOM Helen Bianchin
(Society Weddings)
In her marriage of convenience to Carlo Santangelo, Aysha
knew she'd gain wealth, status and the sexiest husband ever!
Aysha loved her fiancé and wanted a real marriage, but would
Carlo give up his glamorous mistress...?

#2068 LOVER BY DECEPTION Penny Jordan
(Sweet Revenge/Seduction)
When Anna Trewayne lost her memory, she mistakenly
believed Ward Hunter to be a friend and lover. She'd
welcomed him into her arms...her bed...but what would
happen when her memory returned?

#2069 A MARRIAGE BETRAYED Emma Darcy
Kristy longed to find her natural family, but instead she found
Armand Dutournier, who wanted revenge for a betrayal she
hadn't committed. Did that mean she had a twin? Was he the
only lead to the family she yearned for?

#2070 THE YULETIDE CHILD Charlotte Lamb
(Expecting!)
Dylan had been thrilled when she'd married handsome
Ross Jefferson after a whirlwind romance. But she'd also
moved out of town and become unexpectedly pregnant.
Worse—her husband seemed to be having an affair....

#2071 MISTLETOE MISTRESS Helen Brooks
Joanne refused to have an affair with her sexy, arrogant
boss, Hawk Mallen. But then he offered her a dream
promotion—with one catch: she was at his command day
and night. Could she resist such a tempting proposal?

#2072 THE FAITHFUL WIFE Diana Hamilton
Jake and Bella, once happily married, have been separated a
whole year. Now Jake and Bella are tricked into spending
Christmas together. Isolated, they discover the passion is
still there—but can they overcome their past?